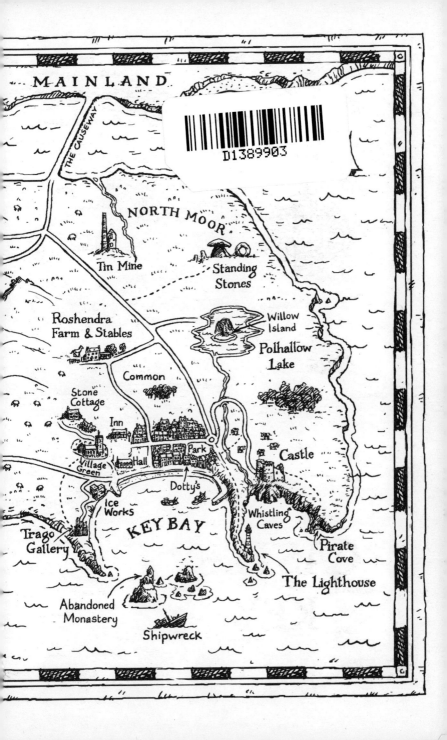

Collect all the Adventure Island *books*

ADVENTURE ISLAND
THE MYSTERY OF THE MIDNIGHT GHOST

Helen Moss

Illustrated by Leo Hartas

Orion
Children's Books

First published in Great Britain in 2011

by Orion Children's Books
a division of the Orion Publishing Group Ltd
Orion House
5 Upper St Martin's Lane
London WC2H 9EA
An Hachette UK company

1 3 5 7 9 10 8 6 4 2

A catalogue record for this book is
available from the British Library.

ISBN 978 1 4440 0329 1

Printed in Great Britain by Clays Ltd, St Ives plc

For Amy and Beth

One

An Exciting Arrival

'You'll *never* guess who's just checked in at The Lighthouse!' Emily shouted into her mobile phone, before Scott even had a chance to say hello.

'Nelson Mandela?' Scott suggested. 'David Beckham? No, don't tell me, the Queen . . .'

Emily laughed. The boys would never guess in a million years! She jumped up and grabbed her binoculars from the box marked *Operations Kit* under her bed. There were three windows in the curved walls of her bedroom, all small and round like a ship's portholes. One looked out to a sky full of seagulls and a sparkling blue sea stretching to the horizon. The next framed Key Bay with its towering cliffs, topped by the jagged outline of the castle ruins. But it was the third window she ran to now, with its view of Castle Key far below, tiny as a model village. Tucked behind the church she could make out Stone Cottage, where her new friends Scott and Jack Carter were spending the summer with their Aunt Kate. Having your bedroom on the top floor of a lighthouse was a definite plus for all-round surveillance!

'Lady Gaga? Johnny Depp?' It was Jack's voice now. Emily pictured him wrestling the phone out of his older brother's hand. 'Winnie the Pooh?'

Winnie the Pooh? If Jack was moving on to *fictional* characters, they could be here for weeks! Emily couldn't bear it any longer – it was like giving someone an amazing Christmas present and then having to watch while they opened it in slow motion, trying not to tear the paper. 'It's an ex-SAS commando,' she blurted.

'Yeah, right!' Scott had grabbed his phone back from Jack. 'And I suppose James Bond will be popping in later for your mum's buffet lunch!'

Emily was used to Scott teasing her. She did a

backwards dive onto her bed. 'His name's Max Fordham. He was in the Gulf War and he's done loads of secret operations.' Then she screamed as a blur of black and tan and white fur launched itself onto her stomach. 'Drift! It's not a game,' she giggled. A rescue dog of unknown origin, Drift was the perfect combination of the best bits of every breed – the brains of a collie, the bounce of a spaniel, the bravado of a Jack Russell – and he was Emily's constant companion.

In the sunny kitchen at Stone Cottage, Scott shook his head at his mobile and grinned at his brother. 'According to Em, a member of the SAS has just checked in at The Lighthouse.'

'SAS? As in Special Air Service?' Jack spluttered through a mouthful of bacon. It was still early and they were working their way through one of Aunt Kate's immense cooked breakfasts. 'As in *Who Dares Wins* and all that? Cool!'

Scott shrugged. Emily was always imagining secret agents, kidnappers and gangsters around every corner! If Winnie the Pooh *did* turn up at her parents' Bed and Breakfast at The Lighthouse, Emily would suspect him of masterminding an international honey-smuggling ring. Her SAS commando was probably just a guy with muscles in camo-pattern trousers.

'How do you *know* he's SAS?' Scott asked, switching

his phone to speaker so that Jack could hear. 'Did he storm in through the window brandishing a machine gun?'

'When he was signing the register I noticed he had this little tattoo on his arm,' Emily explained patiently. 'A dagger with wings on it. That's the SAS insignia.'

Scott had to admit he was impressed. Emily noticed things. She noticed things most people wouldn't notice even if they were waving a red flag and doing a Mexican Wave.

'So I asked him,' Emily went on, 'and he told me all about it. He's really nice. Drift likes him too!' As far as Emily was concerned Drift was never wrong about such things.

'But what's he doing in Castle Key?' Scott asked. 'They haven't discovered a terrorist cell operating out of Dotty's Tea Rooms have they?'

'I told you, Max isn't in the SAS any more. He's a civilian now.' Emily shook her head. Sometimes talking to the boys could be like walking up a down escalator!

In the kitchen at Stone Cottage, Jack let a piece of bacon fall off his fork. 'So he's just here on *holiday*? Yawn!'

'Ah, but I haven't told you the Most Amazing Part of All yet!' Emily said in a mysterious tone. 'Meet me at the end of the harbour wall in ten minutes.'

Scott did a double take at his phone. Emily had rung off already. He raised his eyebrows in Jack's direction.

But Jack was already at the door. Bubbles of excitement were fizzing in his stomach. If Emily said something was *amazing*, it was *guaranteed to* be good! Then he ran back into the kitchen and snagged a piece of toast to eat on the way. 'What are we waiting for?' he asked, tugging Scott by the scruff of his t-shirt.

'Calm down!' Scott got up from his chair with all the speed of a sleep-walking snail. Scott liked to appear ice-cool and unruffled in all situations. It drove Jack crazy! Especially when he knew that beneath the laid-back pose, Scott was just as keen to find out Emily's news as he was.

The boys headed down Church Lane, along the high street, and through Fish Alley onto the seafront. The narrow streets of the old fishing village were familiar territory now, although Scott and Jack had only arrived in Castle Key a few weeks ago. They'd been packed off to stay with their Great-aunt Kate while Dad was spending the summer at an archaeological site in Africa digging up old pots. At first Jack had thought he'd die of boredom – a million miles from London and his friends – stuck in the middle of nowhere on an island he'd never even heard of off the coast of Cornwall.

But then the boys met Emily Wild, and the next thing they knew, they were swept up in Operation Treasure, tracking down a stolen Saxon sword, helmet and shield. OK, so getting trapped in a pitch black cave in a storm with the tide rising by the second was *not* an experience Jack wanted to repeat any time soon, but the rest of it had been awesome! Since then, things had been a little quiet. They'd been assisting Emily with her ongoing investigation, Operation Spy Ring. Unfortunately, despite the exciting name, it hadn't turned out to have quite the thrill-factor Jack had hoped for, mainly involving staking out the Post Office and watching people buying stamps. It was high time for a new adventure.

The boys hurried along the pebble beach where they were met by Drift, springing around their ankles like a hyperactive grasshopper. Emily was waiting for them, perched on the wall, hugging her knees to her chest, her jumble of long brown curls curtaining her face.

'What's the Most Amazing Part of All?' Jack panted.

Emily grinned at the boys' eager faces. They were already looking less London and more Castle Key; the sun had brought out freckles on Jack's nose and streaked Scott's floppy brown hair with surfer-dude highlights. 'You've heard of the Agent Diamond films, right?'

'*Heard* of them!' Jack laughed, sitting down next to Emily on the limpet-encrusted wall. 'They're only my all-time favourite movies! *The Diamond Mission* was the best. That's the one where Maya Diamond has to find Dr Zoltan's secret underwater lair . . .'

'No way!' Emily shoved Jack so he almost toppled backwards off the wall, '*The Diamond Code* was the classic. Where Maya has to go undercover as a double agent in Russia . . .'

Scott laughed and held up his hands. 'Cease fire! We *all* rate the Agent Diamond films, but what have they got to do with your SAS guy?'

Emily shaded her eyes and gazed out across the bay, pausing for maximum effect. 'They're going to film some scenes for the next movie on location here at the castle! Max Fordham is their stunt advisor.'

'*Agent Diamond*? Filming *here*?' Jack echoed. This was *officially* the single most exciting thing that had ever happened in the history of the universe.

'When?' Scott asked. He was trying to sound casual, but Jack could tell he was stoked too.

'They start filming in a couple of days.' Emily hopped down from the wall and started strolling casually away from the harbour. Drift trotted along behind, his velvety ears bobbing up and down in time with his paws.

'Where are you going?' Scott called.

Emily turned and spoke as she continued to walk backwards. 'Max said we could go up to the castle and watch him set up the stunts. That's if you're interested, of course . . .'

'*If* we're interested? Jack laughed. '*If?*' He sprang down from the wall and rocketed after Emily. Scott was not far behind.

Watching an SAS commando rigging up impossibly dangerous stunts for a high-octane action thriller – Jack had never been more interested in anything in his entire life!

Two

Extreme Difficulty

When they reached the top of Castle Road, the friends found the parking area in front of the castle packed with trucks and vans. People were dashing about unloading boxes of ropes, hooks and harnesses or wheeling around cameras, lights and winches. Others were walking backwards holding clipboards and shouting instructions. It was like rush hour in London.

'I bet Key Castle hasn't seen this much action since it

was last invaded in 1385!' Scott exclaimed.

The friends wandered round to the far side of the ruins. The castle was perilously close to the cliff edge, and Jack noticed that safety barriers had been installed to prevent any of the crew accidentally plunging hundreds of feet onto the rocks below.

'Look, there's Max.' Emily pointed up at one of the two corner towers that were still standing. Jack watched, open-mouthed, as a figure in black t-shirt and shorts scaled the crumbling tower as effortlessly as a spider scurrying up a garden fence. Max attached a rope at the top, then descended, swinging from side to side, hammering in bolts, attaching ropes and testing hand- and foot-holds as he went. Reaching the ground, he unclipped from the rope and began discussing camera angles with the construction team who were putting up a platform at the base of the tower.

'Wow!' Jack breathed. 'That beats the climbing wall in the school gym any day.'

They watched enthralled until Max told his crew to take a break. Then he pulled off his helmet and jogged over to where the friends were sitting on the grass, pushing his aviator sunglasses up over his short dark hair. His steely blue eyes looked as if they'd spent a lot of time squinting through the sights of a gun in the glare of the desert sun.

'These are my friends, Scott and Jack,' Emily said. Max gave a friendly nod and high-fived with them all. Jack caught a glimpse of the winged dagger tattoo on his arm.

'That was cool!' Jack said. 'The way you free-climbed that wall.'

'Cheers. Are you a climber yourself?' Max asked.

Jack nodded. He loved climbing.

Max grinned. 'I started when I was your age. Then I did a lot in the army, of course.'

'Have you ever climbed an E9?' Jack asked.

'Yeah, a few. On El Cap in California, a bunch in the Alps, New Zealand . . .'

'Wow!' Jack was in awe. E9 was the highest confirmed grade of Extreme Difficulty in rock climbing. He'd watched videos on the internet of famous climbers scaling them, but to actually *meet* someone who'd nailed loads of them was something else.

'Hey, if you guys are up for it,' Max offered, 'I could take you out for a climbing session at the end of the week when I'm done here.'

Jack exchanged grins with Scott and Emily. This day was just getting better and better.

Max called to one of the crew who was pushing around a little cart with a cool box. 'Could we get some drinks over here please, Daisy?' He fished cans of Coke from the ice and handed them round. 'And can you rustle up a bowl of water for my little friend?' he added. Drift wagged not just his tail, but his entire body from the collar down.

Scott laughed. The little dog had nearly as severe a case of advanced Hero-Worship Syndrome as Jack and Emily. But it had to be said, Max Fordham was, without doubt, one of the coolest guys on the planet, even by Scott's high standards of Cooldom. 'Thanks for letting us watch you set up,' he said. 'What's going to happen in this stunt?'

Max Fordham took a long swig from his Coke. 'Maya Diamond is going to escape from the castle. She abseils down the wall of the tower – using the ropes that Dr Zoltan's henchmen tied her up with. Then she deadhangs off the cliff face, does a back flip, inches along a ledge and leaps out, grabbing on to the landing skids of a passing helicopter. We can do a lot with computer graphics now, but we try to keep it real as possible on Agent Diamond . . . ' Max glanced at his watch. 'Well, good talking to you but I've got to crack on. I want to have the castle wall prepped for filming tomorrow.'

'Tomorrow?' Scott echoed. 'Does that mean that *Savannah Shaw* will be here?' He deliberately ignored the little smirk flickering across Jack's face. Jack had teased Scott about having a crush on Savannah Shaw – the actress who played Maya Diamond – ever since Scott had stupidly admitted he thought she was 'pretty'.

'No.' Max crushed his coke can in his fist and shook his head. 'Savannah doesn't do her own stunts. It'll be her body-double, Lauren O'Brien.'

Jack couldn't help feeling disappointed. He'd always thought Savannah Shaw was like Superwoman or Lara Croft or something. 'Is Savannah too scared to do them herself?'

'No. It's not Savannah's fault. She'd love to do her

own stunts, but her agent and the film company won't let her.' There was a weary edge to Max's voice and a muscle twitched along his jaw. 'She's far too *valuable* for them to risk anything happening to her. I sometimes think the poor girl gets treated like a piece of priceless crystal instead of a human being.'

Jack's face fell. 'Sorry, I didn't mean . . .'

Max clapped him on the shoulder. 'No, *I'm* sorry, mate. I just get a bit worked up about some of the *sleazier* elements of the film industry! Oh, and talking of the sleazier elements of the film industry, here's one of them now . . .'

A black Ferrari with GOLD-1 on the number-plate screeched into the car park. Scott heard Jack whistle an admiring 'Whoah! Nice wheels!'

A man the size and shape of a small walrus squeezed out of the driving seat. Before his feet had even touched the ground, he was barking for someone to bring him a double-shot espresso *immediately.*

'Sid Golding!' Max spat out the words as if they tasted of rancid pickled onions. 'He's Savannah Shaw's agent. Savannah was only seventeen when she was selected for the first Agent Diamond movie. Golding has "looked after" her career from the start.'

The walrus was now striding towards them. He was wearing a sharp grey suit that looked very Italian and very expensive. 'What's going on here? We need this set ready *yesterday*!'

Max narrowed his piercing eyes and raised one eyebrow a fraction. 'It's all under control.'

'It'd better be!' Golding scowled at Scott, Jack and Emily. 'And we don't need hangers-on getting in the way.'

'My friends are here at my express invitation,' Max said. 'They're big Agent Diamond fans. I'm sure you'll want to make them welcome.'

Sid Golding made a harrumphing noise like a whale spouting water from its blow-hole. Then he snatched the coffee being held out at arm's length by a trembling assistant and marched away.

Max rolled his eyes. 'Golding's totally paranoid about crazed fans getting too close to Savannah, or paparazzi snapping photos of her in her slippers or something!'

'Do we *look* like paparazzi?' Scott grumbled.

'Or crazed fans?' Emily added.

'Speak for yourself,' Jack laughed, contorting his face and lurching around like the Hunchback of Notre Dame. 'I'm crazed. *Crazed*, I tell you!'

Max laughed. 'Well, if you're *that* crazy about her, you might see her at Pendragon Manor. They're filming some scenes there this week as well. Just keep out of Golding's way. Oh, and don't say I sent you.'

'*Pendragon Manor*? But that's only just up the road!' Emily could hardly believe her ears.

Savannah Shaw, aka Agent Maya Diamond, *the most famous female spy in the world*, was coming to the island.

Three

Perfectly Innocent

Pendragon Manor was about four miles from Castle Key village and the friends planned to cycle. The boys had brought their bikes with them from London on the back of Dad's car. But next morning, Jack was greeted with a major disaster. The back wheel of his trusty BMX bike was twisted. It must have happened when he'd been practicing his three-sixties in Church Lane the other day. He phoned the bike shop in

Carrickstowe and they said they'd order a new wheel for him, but it would take several days.

'Never mind, dear. There's an old bike in the garden shed that your dad used to whizz around on when he was a boy.' Aunt Kate wiped her hands on her apron and fastened a wisp of her fluffy white hair back into one of her many hair grips. 'I'll make you a picnic, shall I?'

That's the best thing about Aunt Kate, Jack thought. *She understands the importance of food supplies for a successful mission.*

The bike was black and dusty and as heavy as a tank. It wasn't *exactly* a Penny Farthing, but it was a close relative. Jack clambered on and lurched round the garden. The handlebars were so high they were almost round his ears.

'Smile!' Scott called.

Jack looked round. His foot caught in the pedal and the next thing he knew he was lying in a flowerbed locked in an embrace with ten tonnes of Stone Age bicycle.

'Perfect timing!' Scott laughed, snapping a photo on his mobile phone. 'This is going on Facebook. Your mates are going to love it. Jack BMX-Champion Carter falling off a granny bike!'

'Paparazzi!' Jack fumed, extracting rose thorns from his shorts. He had to get hold of Scott's phone and delete that picture if it killed him.

Emily had her own bike, of course; her dad had customized it with a big basket on the back for Drift. Drift loved bike rides. When they set off half an hour later, free-wheeling down Church Lane, he sat up happily in his basket with his tongue hanging out and his ears streaming back in the wind.

'I hope we don't run into Walrus Guy again,' Jack said as they pedalled out of the village and turned west into a narrow lane bordered by hedges so high they almost met overhead to form a tunnel.

'Me too,' Emily agreed, 'but if we *do* see Sid Golding, stick to the plan. We say we're just going for a perfectly innocent picnic in the woods . . .'

'And if we *just happen* to wander a bit close to the manor,' Scott added, 'and *just happen* to unavoidably catch sight of Savannah Shaw, there's nothing he can do about it.'

'Yeah, it's a free country!' Jack agreed. He attempted to strike a blow for freedom with a defiant wheelie and immediately wished he hadn't. True, he caught some great air, but seconds later he caught a faceful of road too. This bike wasn't built for freestyle tricks. With only one leg-shredding gear, it wasn't built for speed or hills either. In fact, Jack wasn't sure what it *was* built for.

'And of course,' Emily patted the large bag over her shoulder, 'if I *just happen* to have my binoculars with me . . .'

'. . . for a spot of perfectly innocent bird-watching, perhaps?' Jack suggested as he climbed back on The Bike from Hell.

They cycled up a long hill until they stopped for breath at the crest of the ridge. Standing down from the pedals, Emily gazed across the rolling moors towards the ocean, which pounded at the craggy west coast of the island. The bottom of the valley was cloaked in thick woods. A jumble of roofs and chimneys could be seen poking up from the swathes of shadowy green. The rustling of the leaves sounded like whispering voices. 'Pendragon Manor looks spooky even from here,' Emily said.

'What's *spooky* about it?' Jack laughed. 'It looks like your basic big posh house in a wood.'

'Ah, but Pendragon Manor is *haunted*!' Emily announced in her best Horror Movie voice.

'Haunted?' Jack stood up on the pedals and tried bouncing the back wheel. '*Cool!* What by?'

'Duh! A ghost, *obviously!*' Scott rolled his eyes.

Jack gave up on the bounces and kicked out at Scott's shin. 'Well, thank you for that, Einstein! I didn't think it was haunted by a *ham sandwich*, did I? I meant what *kind* of ghost. I hope it's a poltergeist? You know, those ones that trash the place and drive people bonkers. That's what I want to come back as . . .'

'*Come back as?*' Scott laughed. 'You do all that already!'

Emily grinned. 'The ghost at Pendragon Manor is much classier than a poltergeist. She's a witch.'

'Really? The ghost of a witch?' Scott asked. He leaned forward and rested his elbows on his handlebars. 'You're making it up!'

Emily shook her head and smiled mysteriously. '*Everyone* in Castle Key knows about the legend of the Midnight Ghost. Most people refuse to go anywhere near the manor after dark.'

'So what is this legend?' Jack demanded.

Emily closed her eyes and swayed as if she'd gone into a trance. 'Let me take you back in time to the sixteenth century,' she intoned. 'There were strange goings-on at Pendragon Manor. Young women kept vanishing mysteriously after spending a night there. People accused the old housekeeper, Sarah Goodwell, of being a witch and cursing the missing girls. When the manor was searched, they found a secret attic room full of spellbooks and magic potions. Sarah Goodwell was dragged away and hanged. But the legend says she used one of her own spells to keep her spirit alive to wreak revenge. Her ghost still prowls that attic room and it is said that if any girl or woman enters after midnight, she'll disappear, never to be seen again!' Emily opened her eyes and stared dramatically at the boys.

There was a long silence. '*That. Is. So. Awesome!*' Jack breathed eventually. 'A real live ghost! Well, not *live*, obviously. A real, *dead* ghost! We have *got* to stay the night in that room. I've always wanted to see a ghost. We'll need some garlic and a cross . . .'

Scott slapped his palm to his forehead. 'That's *vampires*, you lamebrain!'

Emily laughed. At least she aimed for a laugh but it came out more like a squeak. She'd been trying to freak the boys out with the ghost story but had succeeded in giving *herself* the creeps! She had to admit, the Midnight Ghost was a bit scary. She'd even had nightmares about it when she was little. Drift didn't help by whimpering and doing his Frightened Ears – pressed back flat against his head. He'd detected the trace of fear in her laugh, of course. It was impossible to hide *anything* from Drift.

Emily laughed again and shook her head at her own silliness. 'Come on,' she said, 'we're going to see *Savannah Shaw*, remember? Now, *she's* a real legend. Much better than some old ghost!' She took off down the hill, letting the wind blow away her heebie-jeebies like cobwebs from brambles.

When they reached the woods the three friends wheeled their bikes along the shady path beneath the oaks and beeches. They trod softly and spoke in whispers, but they soon realized they needn't have bothered; they could've been riding on tap-dancing elephants and no one would've noticed. With trucks and trailers and mechanical rigs parked everywhere, and crowds of people rushing among them, the grounds of Pendragon Manor looked like a giant fairground.

Keeping to the edge of the wood, Emily, Scott and Jack drew closer, until they found themselves behind a tall hedge that encircled the formal gardens. 'This is a perfect Observation Post.' Emily whispered. Then she turned to Drift. 'Stake-out!' The little dog recognized the command instantly and lay down in the bike basket.

They peeped through the branches of the hedge to a striped lawn the size of a cricket pitch. In the centre was a giant maze constructed from clipped yew hedges. The film crew was busy positioning cameras and lights all around it. Emily glanced up at the manor. The original Tudor house of fudge-coloured stone had been added to over the years with a hodge-podge of extra wings and. towers and turrets. It even *looked* like a haunted house from a horror movie.

'Look, it's *her*!' Scott whispered.

Emily turned to look. A beautiful woman was gliding across the lawn, dressed in a tight black Ninja-style catsuit. She was wearing designer sunglasses and her glossy dark hair was pulled back into a long ponytail, showing off her cut-glass cheekbones. She was sipping from a bottle of water and toting an enormous, mean-looking laser gun over her shoulder. Assistants wielding hairdryers and make-up brushes followed in her wake, along with a man waving an electric fan about and a beefy bodyguard sporting an FBI-style earpiece.

Emily was spellbound. For a moment she forgot all about her dream of training as a top MI5 agent. She wanted to be Savannah Shaw – travelling the world, starring in films, having people running around after her . . .

But suddenly Emily's daydream was interrupted. With a scrabble and a thud, Drift was out of the basket. She grabbed for his collar but it was too late. He was through the hedge and tearing across the lawn like a heat-seeking missile. Time stood still and she could only watch in horror as Drift made directly for Savannah Shaw. The bodyguard and the man with the fan both threw themselves to the ground to intercept the canine intruder, but they only succeeded in a head-on collision with each other. Meanwhile Drift jumped up and planted his little paws as high up on Savannah Shaw's Ninja legs as he could reach.

At the same moment, a walrus-shaped man in a sharp suit came storming across the lawn. His face glistened heart-attack red; you could almost see the steam coming out of his ears.

'Drift!' Emily gulped.

'Sid Golding!' Scott groaned.

Jack closed his eyes. 'Oh, we are in so much trouble now!'

Four

Meeting with a Legend

'WHAT IS THE MEANING OF THIS?' Sid Golding bellowed. He clapped his hand over his eyes. 'Someone tell me I'm hallucinating. There *CANNOT BE* a rabid animal savaging my talent!' He lifted his hand and glowered down at the bodyguard and the man with the fan, who were still lying flat-out on the lawn. 'GET UP, YOU IMBECILES!' He pulled a mobile phone from his shirt pocket and began stabbing at it with a podgy forefinger. 'I'm calling my lawyers. We'll sue the *pants* off the owners! Someone call an ambulance; Savannah could have been bitten. And someone remove this . . . *mongrel*!'

Scott watched, clutching his hair so tightly in both hands it was starting to hurt. This was the biggest disaster since that incident last year involving Jack, a rugby ball and next-door's new widescreen TV!

'I'm going to rescue Drift,' Emily said.

'No, hang on,' Jack grabbed Emily's elbow and pointed through the hedge. 'Look, Savannah's got him.'

Scott could hardly believe his eyes. Savannah Shaw, one of the most *legendary* film stars in the galaxy, had scooped Drift up in her arms. This was like Kiera Knightley popping round to feed your goldfish, or Angelina Jolie cleaning out your gerbil cage – *it didn't happen.*

—

'Chill out, Sid!' Savannah's voice was soft and bubbled with laughter. She sounded much more human than her ice-cool on-screen character, Maya Diamond. 'This little guy's not doing any harm.' She kissed Drift's fur. 'And the only ones round here who need medical attention are Larry and Kenzo!' She glanced down at the two men on the ground, who were now sitting up rubbing their heads. 'I think they had a meeting of minds. You OK, guys?' she added.

Sid Golding bobbed up and down on the spot spluttering like an unexploded firework. 'You look tense, Sid,' Savannah said kindly. 'Why don't you go lie down and have Ingrid massage your feet?'

Golding's rage began to fizzle out. 'Yeah, I'm gonna do that. This stress has brought my ankles up again.' He turned and glared at the film crew. 'Savannah needs to take a time-out.' He clapped his hands. '*Ingrid!* Feet! *Someone!* Double-shot espresso!'

Savannah smiled. 'I'd like to sit in the shade of that hedge over there.' She pointed at the very spot that concealed the three friends, their bikes and a dog-basket.

'Oh, no, we're toast!' Jack whispered. 'Burnt toast with melted chee—'

'*Shhhhh,*' Scott and Emily hissed.

Savannah Shaw sat down on the folding chair that had been magically provided by her army of assistants – along with a table and mirrors for the make-up artist. She shrugged the laser gun from her shoulder and lowered Drift onto the grass. Then she poured mineral water from her bottle into a plastic tray she found on the make-up table – first tipping out the cotton wool balls. The little dog gazed up at Savannah. His ears – both the black one and the white one with brown spots – were sticking out almost horizontally. Emily couldn't help feeling a twinge of jealousy. In Drift-language those ears meant only one thing: *I love you even more than biscuits!* And it was an expression he usually reserved exclusively for Emily.

Scott *almost* allowed himself to breathe again; maybe they wouldn't be spotted after all . . .

Savannah took a silk scarf from her jacket pocket and wiped a paw-print from her leg. She pushed her sunglasses up onto her forehead to reveal her trademark emerald green eyes, and smiled at one of the assistants fussing around her. 'Would you mind bringing me three more chairs? I'm expecting visitors.'

Then she turned to the hedge and winked.

Scott stared. *OK, now I must be losing it – for one crazed moment I thought Savannah Shaw winked at me!* But, there it was again. Those long silky lashes definitely fluttered shut over the sparkling green of her right eye. *No! She must have something in her eye.*

Then she spoke. 'It's OK. You can come out now. Sid's gone.'

Scott looked at Jack and Emily. Jack and Emily looked at Scott.

An Ice Age passed. Then another. 'Er, you mean *us*?' Scott croaked eventually.

Savannah Shaw giggled. 'Unless there's anyone *else* hiding behind that hedge.'

In a hypnotic trance, Scott let his bike fall to the ground and crawled under the hedge.

Savannah Shaw smiled at him. 'Have a seat!'

Maya Diamond just spoke to me! Maybe he was

dreaming? If so, he hoped he didn't wake up for a very long time! Not that he had a *crush* on her, of course . . .

Emily and Jack emerged from under the hedge. 'Oh, I'm so sorry, Miss Shaw,' Emily said. 'Drift has never run off like this before.'

'It's OK. He's adorable. And please, call me Savannah. I love dogs! I have a labradoodle called Scrumble at my ranch in California.' Savannah Shaw smiled but there was a sad, faraway look in her beautiful eyes. 'I'm travelling so much I hardly see him. I have staff to look after him, but it's not the same . . .'

Drift shuffled over to Emily, head to one side, tail wagging so sheepishly that Emily couldn't be cross. She gave him a big hug. Then she looked at the boys. They'd both lost the power of speech and were gawping at Savannah Shaw as if a unicorn or a mermaid had just appeared in front of their eyes.

'But how did you know we were there?' Emily asked.

'When Drift came hurtling across the lawn, I noticed that he came through that hole in the bottom of the hedge. And Max Fordham told me he'd made friends with the lighthouse keeper's daughter and her little dog and her two friends, so I put two and two together.'

Emily was impressed. Savannah may not sound like Maya Diamond, and she may not do her own stunts, but she *thought* like a secret agent!

'So, what are you guys up to for the rest of the day?' Savannah asked.

'Perfectly innocent picnic in the woods!' Jack recited in a robotic voice, like a soldier sticking to his story under interrogation.

'That sounds like fun. I wish I could go off for a picnic instead of filming all day. I've got to fight off half a dozen of Dr Zoltan's henchmen in the maze, and then there's a love scene with Brett diBlanco to look forward to.'

From the way she wrinkled her nose, Emily got the distinct impression that Savannah wasn't actually looking forward to it very much at all. Emily sympathized. Even though he was one of the biggest heart-throb actors around, and all the girls at school were gaga about him, Emily secretly thought Brett diBlanco looked a bit slimy.

'Hey, do you guys know this place is meant to be haunted?' Savannah asked. 'I *love* anything to do with ghosts. Not just silly Halloween spooks. I mean ghosts of real people in historic buildings.'

Emily was so excited to be chatting with Savannah Shaw that she happily recounted the legend of the Midnight Ghost for the second time that morning. This time she did it without the fake trance and spooky voice effects.

'Wow! That is so neat. The ghost of a witch!' Savannah turned in her chair and glanced up at the manor house. 'I wonder which of those windows belongs to the haunted attic . . .'

Emily looked up and couldn't help a little shiver. Pendragon Manor was such a creepy-looking place you could almost imagine there really *were* ghosts wandering around up there. Suddenly, her heart pounded as if it were trying to break out of her ribcage; a shadowy figure had appeared at one of the little diamond-paned windows tucked under the roof and it was now staring out across the garden straight at them.

Emily grabbed Scott's arm. 'Look!' she said, her voice quavering. 'There's someone up in that attic room.'

'Oooh, where?' Savannah asked excitedly. She, Scott and Jack all looked up at the window where Emily was pointing.

But the figure had gone.

'Ha ha,' Jack laughed. 'Nice try!'

Emily gulped. She was *sure* she'd seen a dark figure in the window. But she must have imagined it. She shrugged and laughed it off. 'Yeah, got you going there, didn't I?'

'Sorry, Savannah, but I need to take off your mouth and start again.' The make-up artist – a thin woman with bleached blonde hair and a necklace that looked like it was made from liquorice allsorts – dabbed at Savannah's face with a sponge. 'You've totalled your lipstick kissing the little dog.' Then she grinned. 'And you can't do the snog scene with Brett with dog hair on your face. He's allergic. He'd be sneezing for the rest of the day.'

Savannah smiled and said something under her breath. Emily couldn't be sure but it sounded a lot like, *Don't tempt me, Megan!*

'Two minutes, people!' The shout came over a megaphone.

'Uh-oh,' Savannah groaned. 'That's the director. I'd better say goodbye and get my mouth back on. It's been great meeting you all. Enjoy your picnic . . .'

As Emily stood up she noticed the scarf Savannah had used to wipe away Drift's paw-prints lying on the grass. She picked it up and held it out.

Savannah smiled. 'You keep it. That blue sets off your pretty chestnut hair.'

Clutching the scarf, Emily squeezed back through the hedge after the boys. She was settling Drift back in his basket when the director's voice boomed out again. 'Savannah Shaw on set NOW! We've got a scene to shoot here.'

'Story of my life,' Savannah muttered on the other side of the hedge.

Maybe being a film star isn't so great, Emily thought. She would stick to MI5 after all.

Five

The Scent of Mystery

Next morning Scott and Jack met Emily and Drift at Dotty's Tea Rooms to plan a trip to the water park in Carrickstowe. It was another scorching day and they took their ice creams outside and sat at a pavement table under the shade of a parasol.

'Hey, isn't that Megan?' Emily asked.

Scott glanced up from his blueberry sundae. A group of people were strolling along the seafront towards the café. 'Megan?' Scott didn't recognise her at first, but then he noticed the necklace made out of plastic liquorice allsorts, and it clicked. She was Savannah Shaw's make-up artist.

Jack licked caramel sauce off his spoon and used it as a pointer. 'And that's the man with the fan . . .'

'Kenzo,' Emily prompted.

'Yeah, that's it. He's got an epic black eye,' Jack said with a grimace. 'That bodyguard he crashed into yesterday must have had a hard head.'

'Larry,' Emily said.

Scott grinned. As well as her Powers of Observation, Emily also prided herself on her Memory for Names. He felt sorry for anyone who was ever in a police line-up when she was a witness; they wouldn't stand a chance.

'Ooh, they're coming here,' Jack said. 'Quick, hide under the table, Drift. That Kenzo guy probably isn't your number one fan!'

'Stop staring with your mouth open,' Scott hissed. Sometimes his brother could be more embarrassing than having a zit the size of Wembley stadium on the end of your nose. 'I can see chocolate ice cream on your tonsils and it's grossing me out!'

'I wonder why they're not on set,' Emily whispered. 'I thought they were filming all week.'

Megan recognized the friends and waved as she piled into the café with the rest of the crew. They re-emerged a few minutes later with trays of coffees and cakes and settled down at a nearby table. 'Home-made scones with clotted cream!' Megan enthused. 'Must be about six million calories on this plate! Don't you just *love* Cornwall?'

'And red checked tablecloths! Very retro, darling,' Kenzo laughed.

Scott grinned at Jack and Emily. The new arrivals were so loud, it would be impossible not to overhear their conversation without wearing ear-protectors – even above the squabbling of the seagulls circling overhead in the hope of crumbs.

Megan raised her cappuccino in a toast. 'Well, here's to Savannah. Her mysterious disappearance has given us the morning off.'

Mysterious disappearance? Emily's ears pricked up. Had something suspicious happened? Something that needed *investigating* perhaps? She exchanged glances with Scott and Jack, then focused her attention on the film crew's conversation, trying not to make it *too* obvious she was listening in.

'Of course, Golding's going around telling everyone Savannah's been kidnapped by some lunatic fan who's obsessed with Maya Diamond!' Megan laughed.

Kenzo snorted into his iced coffee. 'I don't know *what* he's getting his boxers in a bundle about. So she didn't turn up on set this morning? Like *that's* never happened before!'

'Well, I heard that Golding's called the police in already,' a man Emily recognized as Savannah's hairdresser piped up. 'She's only been gone two hours! They're hardly going to declare a State of Emergency, are they?'

Emily couldn't contain her curiosity any longer. She got up and went over to Megan's table. 'Sorry, I couldn't help overhearing. You don't think anything *bad* could have happened to Savannah, then?'

Megan shook her head and stirred froth into her cappuccino. 'Poor kid probably just wanted a bit of peace and quiet. She'll have popped on her sunnies and a big hoodie and gone walkabout. It wouldn't be the first time! Bet she's sitting in some little café just like this, pigging out on scones and cream. Golding's had her on a strict lettuce-leaf diet ever since that bikini-shot in the papers showed half a millimetre of fat on her hips . . . '

'Or maybe she's having a *romantic* walk on the beach with Brett?' Kenzo winked. Then he grimaced and touched his fingers to his black eye.

'More likely with Soldier Boy?' the hairdresser chimed in. 'I've seen those two together a few times . . .'

Megan shrugged and bit into her scone. 'Who knows? I'm just happy to have a break from filming.'

The film crew moved onto another topic of gossip. Emily left them to it and re-joined the boys.

'No big deal, then?' Jack returned to the important

business of finishing his ice cream. He was glad, of course, that Savannah hadn't been kidnapped by a psycho-fan or abducted by aliens or anything, but he couldn't help feeling just the teeniest smidgeon of disappointment too. For a moment he thought he'd detected the scent of another mystery in the air. Now the only thing he could smell was the whiff of fish. A fleet of small fishing boats had moored on the other side of the harbour wall and were unloading their mackerel catch. Their friend Old Bob was hauling in a net. Jack waved. The old fisherman touched a gnarled hand to his woollen cap.

Then Jack spotted another familiar face. Mrs Loveday was one of those people it was hard to miss! The caretaker of the Castle Museum was pedalling along the seafront at maximum velocity, wearing a pink child's bike helmet over her grey curls and an orange high-visibility vest over her dress. Since Jack had last seen her – during the investigation into the stolen Saxon treasure – she'd added a Union Jack flag to her bike trailer full of vacuum cleaners and mops.

Jack made a siren noise under his breath. 'Danger! Danger! Incoming Busybody Alert!'

Emily giggled. 'Oh, hello, Mrs Loveday.'

'Hello, dears!' Mrs Loveday hopped down from her bike and smiled at Scott and Emily. For some reason Jack could never fathom, she'd taken a dislike to him from the start, and – as always – glared at him now as if he were a nasty mark on the carpet she'd like to take her scrubbing brush to. 'Ooh, I'm gasping for a cuppa,' she announced. 'It's all very well having these celebrities filming up at the castle, but they do make a mess! And those *Pepperoni* flashing their cameras . . . '

'You mean *paparazzi*?' Scott asked politely.

Jack hid a laugh under a cough. He didn't know how the other two kept a straight face when Mrs Loveday came out with one of her classic mix-ups!

Mrs Loveday didn't even pause for breath. ' . . . they've churned up the gravel in the car park something rotten. And Coke cans and coffee cups everywhere! I said to that Max Fordham, you film stars might get away with it in Hollywood, but in Castle Key we have certain *standards* . . . '

'Max Fordham isn't a film star,' Emily pointed out. 'He was in the SAS.'

'Well, he should know better then! I'm sure they teach them to pick up their litter in the SAS. They certainly did when my Kevin was in the Scouts.'

Jack was almost crying with laughter now.

Mrs Loveday narrowed her eyes at him.

'Sorry, er, it's just that . . . ' Jack gasped.

Emily came to the rescue. '. . . Drift's tickling his leg with his tail!'

'Yes, that's it . . . tickling . . . ooh, stop it, Drift!'

Mrs Loveday pursed her lips and planted her hands on her hips. 'Anyway, if you ask me, Max Fordham was more interested in that Suzannah Shaw than picking up litter.'

'*Savannah* Shaw,' Scott corrected.

'Oh, I can't be doing with these new-fangled names!'

'You saw Savannah Shaw at the castle with Max?' Emily asked. 'When *was* this?'

Mrs Loveday took off her helmet and patted her hair. 'About seven o'clock last night. Round the back of the tower, they were. You know me, I can't *abide* tittle-tattle and I'm not one to Jump to Confusions, but . . .'

Jack noticed that Megan and Kenzo's table were all staring at Mrs Loveday, mouths gaping, like a nest of baby birds waiting to be fed. The film crew clearly liked a gossip themselves, but now they were silent in the presence of a Grand Master. 'Ooh! What were they *doing*?' Megan asked.

Mrs Loveday folded her arms and smiled. 'Well, put it this way, dear, I don't think they were admiring the sunset . . . Savannah Shaw was in his arms!'

Six

Operation Lost Star

Emily sprang up from her chair. 'Come on! Don't want to be late, do we?'

'Late for *what*?' Jack asked.

'You know!' Emily hissed. Then she waved goodbye to Mrs Loveday and hurried off along the seafront with Drift trotting behind her.

Jack wolfed down the last spoon of chocolate ice cream and shrugged at Scott. 'Yeah, better not be *late*.'

Emily darted up Fish Alley and didn't stop until she came to the park at the end of the high street, where she ran up to an enormous old oak tree and disappeared.

'Where'd she go?' Jack panted.

'Up here!' Emily called. Jack and Scott looked up to see Emily reclining on a wide branch, hidden from view by the canopy of leaves. They scrambled up to join her. Drift stood guard below.

Jack made himself comfortable. It was deliciously cool out of the sun. And you could peep out through the foliage and spy on everyone in the park *and* on the high street. Emily had awesome secret hideouts dotted all over the island, ready for any occasion. Although Jack wasn't exactly sure what the occasion *was* this time.

'So, Em, what exactly are we late *for*?' he asked. 'Have you got a meeting with a crack team of undercover squirrels you forgot to mention?'

'I was just making an excuse to get away,' Emily spoke slowly as if explaining quantum physics to a retarded hamster. 'So we can plan our *investigation*.'

'What investigation?' Jack felt as if he'd turned over two pages at once and lost the plot.

'Savannah Shaw has gone *missing*!' Emily pulled her notebook out of her shoulder bag, opened it to a fresh page and wrote *OPERATION LOST STAR*. She underlined it twice.

'But you heard Megan and her mates,' Scott said. 'She's probably just gone off shopping.'

Emily chewed on her pen. 'That's *one* possibility, yes.' She wrote in her notebook again: *1) Gone walkabout??????*

Scott stared at the six question marks. Emily never accepted a simple explanation if a complicated one – preferably involving smugglers or spies – could be found instead. But it had to be said, searching for a film star would be *way* more exciting than staking out the Post Office, even if Savannah *did* turn up scoffing a burger and fries in McDonald's. 'What about Sid Golding's theory?' he suggested. 'That Savannah's been kidnapped by an obsessed fan?'

Emily nodded and wrote, *2) Kidnapped by fan?*

Jack thought he'd enter into the spirit of things. 'Devoured by zombies? Carried off by a hoard of mutant Cornish pixies?'

'*Piskeys!*' Emily corrected.

But Jack was on a roll now. 'Maybe she's been vaporized by that Midnight Ghost?'

'*Vaporized?*' Scott snorted. 'Ghosts don't *vaporize* people!'

Jack shrugged. 'Whatever.'

Emily couldn't help a shudder at the word *ghost,* as she remembered that dark figure at the attic window. But she knew she was being silly. It was probably just a cleaner or something. She looked at Jack and laughed. 'I'm not even going to bother to write that down!'

'Cheers!' Jack said. 'Well, where do *you* think she's

49

gone then? If we *have* to be boring and rule out all forms of supernatural activity . . .'

Emily held up her pen. 'My theory is that Savannah's run off with Max Fordham. Mrs Loveday saw them together at the castle last night . . .'

Jack laughed. 'Mrs Loveday? Gossip Queen of Cornwall? Not exactly a reliable source, is she?'

'And, according to Kenzo, Savannah is dating Brett diBlanco, anyway,' Scott pointed out. 'Which makes sense. She's more likely to be going out with another big-shot film star than a soldier.'

Emily leapt to Max's defense. 'But Max Fordham is *way* better looking and cooler than Brett diBlanco.' She snapped her mouth shut, realizing – nanoseconds too late – that she might as well have taken her pen and written PLEASE MAKE FUN OF ME across her forehead!

'Ooooh,' Scott whistled, 'I think Em's in lurrrve with Max Fordham herself!'

'*Max and Emily sitting in a tree! K- I- S- S- I- N- G!*' Jack chanted.

Jack and Scott picked themselves up off the ground and brushed off the twigs and leaves. Luckily the branch wasn't very high and the fall had been more surprising than painful. Emily's shove had come out of nowhere!

'Anyway, I'm not just going on Mrs Loveday's evidence,' Emily said, when the boys had climbed back onto the branch. She ticked off the points on her fingers.

'First, Savannah doesn't even like Brett diBlanco. She wrinkled her nose as if she'd rather kiss a raw fish when she mentioned his name. Second, Savannah said yesterday that Max had told her about meeting us already – which means they must have been in touch the evening before. And third, the hairdresser guy said he'd seen them together a few times . . .' Emily folded her arms and leant back against the tree trunk. 'I rest my case.'

Scott laughed. Emily might have an over-active imagination, but you couldn't argue with her logic. 'OK, you win. It's a *possibility*. Add it to the list.'

Emily wrote it down, then snapped her notebook shut. 'Right, let's get moving. The first twenty-four hours of any enquiry are the most important. And if the police aren't even considering this as a Missing Person case yet, we can get a head start.'

'Why don't we head up to the castle?' Scott suggested. 'If your theory's correct, Max Fordham will have gone AWOL too.'

Emily put her hand up for a high-five. 'My thoughts exactly!'

—

'Don't mind me. I'll just die quietly of heat exhaustion . . . ' Jack groaned as they neared the top of Castle Road. It was so hot he'd taken his t-shirt off and wound it round his head like Lawrence of Arabia. *What happened to the water park plan?* That's what he wanted to know.

At the castle, the three friends made their way through the bustling film set until they came to the tower where Max had been working yesterday. There was no sign of him. Emily *knew* she was right; *Max was missing too!* But then a knot of people on the climbing platform moved apart and there he stood – a man in black t-shirt, jeans and aviator sunglasses. Max Fordham.

But what surprised Emily so much she was in danger of falling over backwards was not *only* the fact that Max Fordham was standing there, but that *he was talking to Savannah Shaw*! Emily stared. There was no doubting it. Savannah was in her Maya Diamond costume; slinky black catsuit, long, dark hair in a ponytail, laser gun over her shoulder. Max was standing behind her, saying something into her ear. His arms were wrapped around her waist.

Emily's emotions were in a tailspin. She was relieved that Savannah was safe, of course. At the same time, she couldn't help feeling a bit deflated; Operation Lost Star was over before it'd even begun! Savannah hadn't gone missing after all. She'd just decided to spend the morning with Max watching the stunts being filmed.

Max looked up and waved. Savannah looked up too. But she didn't wave. She didn't even smile. She simply turned away and began to climb the wall.

'Weird! Savannah blanked us. It's like she's a completely different person from the one we met yesterday . . . ' Emily said.

Suddenly Scott laughed. 'That's because she is! Look!'

Emily stared at Savannah, then did a double take. Scott was right. 'Of course!' she cried. 'That's Savannah's stunt double! And Max was just checking her climbing harness was on properly.' Emily couldn't believe she hadn't noticed it before. Lauren O'Brien wasn't as tall as Savannah, for a start. And no wonder she hadn't waved. She'd never met them before!

'I bet that's what Mrs Loveday saw last night too,' Scott said. 'She thought it was Max and Savannah in a snog-fest, but it was just Max and Lauren O'Brien working late on the climbing wall. Talk about *Jumping to Confusions!*'

Emily nodded. 'I suppose we can't really blame Mrs Loveday this time, can we? We were fooled too. In fact, the only one who wasn't taken in was Drift!'

Jack looked down at the little dog. 'What do you mean? He's just sitting there doing nothing. Apart from panting his head off, that is!'

'Exactly!' Emily laughed. 'If that *was* Savannah he'd be over there like a shot like he was yesterday.'

They watched as Max guided Agent Maya Diamond to the top of the wall, then let the rope out slowly for her to come down. When she reached the platform she grinned at Max. 'Just give me 'alf a minute, mate,' she said in an accent that was more South London than Southern California. 'This wig's a nightmare!' She pulled off her long dark hair and scraped both hands through the short, red spiky hair underneath.

Emily looked at the boys. 'So Savannah is still missing. And since Max *is* here, my theory must be wrong. They haven't run off together.'

'Never mind. Look on the bright side,' Scott teased, 'It means he's still available for *you*!' He jumped out of the way to avoid the kick he knew was coming.

But Emily ignored him. 'I guess we'll have to go back to Pendragon Manor and see if she's turned up there.'

'What! *Now?*' Jack groaned. 'What happened to the water park?'

Emily hesitated. Jack was right. It was *roasting*. 'OK, the water park it is! But if Savannah doesn't turn up overnight we'll head out to the manor first thing tomorrow morning.'

Seven

Shocking News

Next morning Emily woke up early and gently eased the snoring Drift from her knees. She couldn't wait to find out whether Savannah Shaw had reappeared or whether they had a full-blown investigation on their hands.

She was spreading Marmite on her toast in the kitchen when Mum came in, wearing a white apron over a tie-dye kaftan, and started loading jugs of milk and plates of fresh fruit on a tray. 'Take this down to the dining room for me, love?' she asked.

Emily was used to the narrow spiral staircase that ran from the top to the bottom of The Lighthouse – all one hundred and twenty steps of it – and had no trouble carrying the heavily-laden tray down from the kitchen to the ground floor. The staircase came out in the huge circular room that served as guest lounge and reception area, and Emily picked a familiar path through the coffee tables and sofas towards the dining room, which was housed in a cheerful conservatory. The morning sun through the porthole windows was dappling the mosaic of bright rugs and Mum's paintings on the wall.

But when Dad came breezing in through the front door with the day's newspapers tucked under his arm, Emily saw something that hit her like a punch in the stomach. The tray slid from her fingers and crashed to the floor.

Dad helped her stagger to a sofa. 'Whatever's the matter? You look as if you've seen a ghost!'

'N-n-n-othing,' Emily stammered. 'It's just that you made me jump.'

Mum appeared in the doorway. Her dark eyes flashed and she snapped her tea towel like a horsewhip. '*Qué lio!*' Mum had lived in England for twenty years and only spoke Spanish when she was either very happy or foot-stampingly furious. And it was obvious she wasn't exactly thrilled at the sight of fruit, milk and smashed crockery all over her favourite rug. 'What a mess!' she yelled, translating, just in case they hadn't got the point the first time.

But then she saw that Emily was almost in tears. She sank onto the sofa and wrapped her in her arms. The thing about Mum was that she could go from a boiling rage to a warm hug in under six seconds. 'Accidents happen,' she said. 'No use crying over spilled milk!'

Dad laughed. 'No use crying over spilled milk – get it?' He looked at the strawberries and blueberries bobbing in their lake of white. 'If you'd wanted to make a smoothie, Emski, couldn't you just have used the blender like everyone else?'

Emily did her best to smile. It was only when she'd finished helping to clear up, and her parents had gone back up to the kitchen, that she was able to run over to the coffee table where Dad had dropped the newspapers and read the terrible headline properly: FILM STAR ABDUCTED BY WITCH GHOST!

With trembling hands, Emily picked up *The Carrickstowe Times* and began to read:

In shock revelations last night, the disappearance of film star Savannah Shaw (24) was linked to a local legend a ghost that haunts Pendragon Manor, where filming for *The Diamond Legacy,* the latest in the blockbuster Agent Diamond series is underway. Miss Shaw's agent, Sid Golding (52), reports that the actress has not been seen since Tuesday morning.

Visibly distressed, Golding told reporters that Savannah Shaw was fascinated by the story of a sixteenth-century witch, Sarah Goodwell, who is said to haunt an attic room at the manor. Local legend has it that any woman who enters the attic after midnight will be cursed by the ghost.

Golding claims that an anonymous witness spotted Savannah Shaw near the haunted room late on Monday night. Miss Shaw's co-star, Brett diBlanco (28) with whom she has been romantically linked, is said to be devastated. Police sources have refused to comment on the case.

Emily closed her eyes and sank back into the cushions. Drift jumped onto her lap and nuzzled his head under her chin. But, for once, even *he* couldn't make things better. Fear and guilt were pulling her down like the tide sucking sand from the shore. *It's all my fault!* Emily thought miserably. *I should never have told her about the Midnight Ghost!*

'Morning!'

Emily jumped and looked up to see Max Fordham on his way to breakfast. She couldn't even manage a smile. Instead she held up *The Carrickstowe Times*. Max smiled and shook his head as he scanned the story.

'Do *you* know where Savannah is?' Emily asked.

'No, I don't!' he said flatly. Emily couldn't tell whether he was amused or annoyed by what he'd read. 'Cursed by a ghost! What a load of twaddle! I wouldn't believe anything Sid Golding says. And as for Brett diBlanco...'

'What about him?' Emily asked. 'The papers are all saying that Brett is Savannah's boyfriend, but she doesn't even *like* him, does she?' Emily still suspected that Max and Savannah were in love, even though Mrs Loveday's sighting had turned out to be a false alarm.

Max shook his head and pretended to zip his mouth. 'No, sorry, I've said too much already.' He sat down and poured himself a coffee.

Emily sighed in frustration, but Max *was* ex-SAS after all. He had clearly been trained to withstand interrogation.

Emily stood in the middle of the guest lounge and gave herself a lecture. Max was right of course. Savannah being cursed by the Midnight Ghost *was* a load of twaddle. She'd totally over-reacted when she saw that headline. There were no such things as ghosts. She'd just imagined that sinister figure at the attic window. There was *obviously* some perfectly rational explanation behind Savannah's disappearance, and Operation Lost Star was going to find out what it was.

—

Meanwhile, at Stone Cottage, Scott and Jack were clearing away their breakfast plates when Aunt Kate's newspaper dropped through the letterbox.

'Uh-oh,' Scott sighed, as he brought it into the

kitchen. 'When Emily sees this stuff about the ghost cursing Savannah she's going to freak out!'

Jack snorted. 'Nah. Em doesn't *really* believe all that stuff. She said so herself. She was just messing about.'

Scott shook his head. He'd noticed that Emily always looked just a tiny bit *wobbly* every time the ghost was mentioned – although she did her best to hide it, of course. And when she said she'd seen a figure at the attic window at Pendragon Manor she'd looked genuinely terrified, even though she'd tried to make a joke of it. 'I just think we should lay off her a bit . . .' he said.

Jack couldn't believe it. Was Scott *seriously* suggesting that Emily believed in ghosts? And if she *did*, were they really going to pass up this prize opportunity to *tease* her about it? He waited for Scott to grin. But he didn't. He was *actually* serious. Jack threw up his hands in surrender. 'OK, you win, just call me Mr Sensitive!'

Secretly, Scott was a bit surprised at himself too. Winding Emily up was usually one of the highlights of his day! *Must be going soft in my old age!* he thought. He pulled out his phone and sent Emily a text. *Meet at the oak tree A.S.A.P.*

—

The boys arrived at the hideout first. Moments later they heard Emily and Drift crunching across the acorns and twigs below.

'First order of business,' Jack called down from the branch, 'I vote we re-name this investigation Operation Ghostbuster!'

Scott poked Jack in the ribs. Hard. *Ghostbuster*? This was his brother's idea of being *sensitive*?

Jack made an innocent face. 'What was that for?'

'You OK, Em?' Scott asked.

Emily scrambled into her place on the branch. 'Fine! Why wouldn't I be?' But she didn't start listing her latest theories or giving out her orders. *She didn't even take her notebook out of her bag!*

She wasn't fine at all.

Scott realized he was going to have to take the lead on this investigation, at least until Emily got a grip again. He didn't have a notebook but he *did* have a voice-recording function on his phone. He spoke into it, ignoring Jack's sniggers. 'Operation Lost Star, Day Two.'

Jack nearly fell out of the tree laughing.

Scott gave up and switched the recorder off. 'OK, let's assume that we're not actually dealing with paranormal activity . . . ' He carefully avoided using the word *ghost* so as not to upset Emily. 'In which case . . .' Scott hesitated after he said *which*, in case Emily heard it as *witch*, but he seemed to have got away with it, '. . . in which case, maybe someone just wants people to *think* Savannah's disappearance is connected to the *you-know-what*.'

'Ooh, ooh!' Jack piped up. 'Like in those old Scooby Doo cartoons where the owner doesn't want people on his land so he tries to scare them off by pretending the place is haunted. It always turns out to be a man with a sheet over his head and a projector.'

'Thank you to Jack Carter for that completely useless input,' Scott muttered. 'If the owner didn't want people on his land he wouldn't have invited a film crew to use it as a location, would he? Now, back in the real world! First, we need to find this nameless witness who supposedly saw Savannah Shaw wandering around the manor in the middle of the night. Who would even *be* in there at night?'

'Cleaners often work at night,' Emily suggested. She was feeling much better now that there was some proper investigating to get her teeth into. She clapped her hands decisively. 'We'll have to go back to Pendragon Manor, track down this witness and check out their story.'

'Just one problem there,' Scott pointed out. 'If Sid Golding catches us he'll sue us, or shoot us, or something!'

Emily smiled. She'd suddenly remembered a small but very useful piece of information. 'Not if we're there to see someone we know!'

'Like who?' Jack asked. 'The only person we "know" there is Savannah and she's been nabbed by a gho—' He felt Scott pinch his arm just in time, '. . . by a g-reat big baddie of totally human and not the tiniest bit supernatural form . . .'

Emily rolled her eyes. 'We know Vicky White,' she said.

'Vicky White?' Jack echoed. Vicky had been working at the Castle Museum when the Saxon treasure was stolen. She'd only been cleared of the crime when Scott, Jack and Emily proved that the real thief had tried to frame her.

'Don't you remember?' Emily said. 'Vicky mentioned that she's got a new job working in the kitchens at Pendragon Manor until she goes back to university?'

'Oh yeah, of course,' Jack fibbed. Like he was ever going to remember that kind of detail! He grinned at Scott. Special Agent Emily Wild was back on form and reporting for duty!

Eight

Making Enquiries

Scott, Jack and Emily left their bikes hidden in a thicket of blackberry bushes at the edge of the woods and crept to their observation post behind the hedge. Although they had a legitimate reason to be at Pendragon Manor this time – Emily had phoned ahead and arranged to meet Vicky – no one was keen on running into Sid Golding again. Drift was tethered on a short lead, in case he got the urge to repeat his greyhound impression and sprint off across the lawn. Not at all impressed with this state of affairs, he kept his ears pointing firmly downwards.

The film set was much quieter today. Cameramen and technicians were mooching about, half-heartedly adjusting equipment. Here and there, people lounged on the grass drinking coffee and checking their mobile phones. It was like a giant waiting room. Without Maya Diamond, there was no Agent Diamond film.

Suddenly Scott noticed a figure scurry into the maze and duck down so he was hidden from the rest of the garden. Tall and stringy as a basketball-player, he was wearing skinny jeans and a checked shirt and carrying a pair of binoculars. He turned to shoot a furtive glance over his shoulder and Scott glimpsed glasses and a straggly goatee beard. 'Hey, that guy could be an obsessed fan . . .' he said.

'Shh!' Emily hissed. 'Walrus Alert!'

Sid Golding was marching out of the huge metal-studded wooden front door of the manor, across the terrace and down a set of wide steps, flanked by a pair of ferocious-looking stone lions, onto the lawn. A group of reporters who'd been hanging around on the terrace leapt up and surrounded him, thrusting their microphones before them like bayonets. Golding broke off from talking urgently into his mobile phone, raised his hands and shouted, 'We are all shocked and deeply concerned for Savannah Shaw's safety. No further comment at this time.' With that, he barrelled across the garden to the drive, jumped into his Ferrari and roared away.

When Scott looked back at the maze, the stalker with the goatee beard had gone.

Moments later an expensively tanned man Emily recognized as Brett diBlanco sashayed across the terrace. He was dressed in a designer polo shirt and tennis shorts so white they looked as though they'd escaped from a washing powder advert. He sat down on a sun-lounger and began leafing through a glossy magazine. The reporters bundled towards him like a rugby pack. He flashed a smile full of dazzling white teeth and began to answer their questions. *For someone who's 'devastated' by his girlfriend's disappearance,* Emily thought, *Brett diBlanco seems to be coping pretty well.*

⌒

Vicky White appeared at the back door to meet the friends, pulling a catering hair net from her strawberry blonde plaits. She wiped her brow with her sleeve. 'Phew! I'm ready for a break. I've been making sandwiches all morning. It's amazing how much that film crew can eat!'

Vicky led the way into a small room off the kitchens, where they sat down around a low table that appeared to have been the scene of a volcanic eruption of dirty

67

coffee cups and biscuit crumbs. 'Staff room,' she laughed. 'This is the bit of the manor that gets left out of the guided tours!'

'Do many people work here?' Emily asked, accepting a can of cola Vicky had rooted out from the back of the fridge.

'Yeah, we do a lot of functions like weddings and conferences. There's about twenty of us in the kitchens.'

Jack decided it was time to cut to the chase. 'What about at night?'

'The cleaners do a night shift. Why, are you guys looking for jobs or something?'

Jack nearly fell off his chair. If he *wanted* a job it'd be something exciting like a sky-diving instructor or Formula One driver. Cleaning old buildings sounded like hard work. 'No way!'

Vicky grinned. 'Come on, I know you're not just here on a social visit. You want to know about Savannah Shaw's disappearance, don't you?'

'It's a fair cop,' Jack admitted.

'So what do you want to know?'

'We want to talk to the *anonymous witness* who saw Savannah Shaw in the manor on Monday night,' Emily said.

Vicky nodded. 'Yeah, that would have to be one of the cleaners.'

'Do you know who was working that night?' Scott asked.

Vicky shook her head, her plaits swinging from side to side. 'Sorry. I don't know any of the night cleaners. They work for an agency in Carrickstowe. A driver brings them over in a van and takes them back again. Most of the locals are too superstitious to work in the manor at night.'

Jack sighed. What a let-down! Their inquiries seemed to have reached a dead end. But then he had a brainwave. 'Can you sneak us in for a reccy round the haunted room?'

Vicky looked at her watch. 'Yeah, if we're quick! I've got a few minutes' break left.'

Emily couldn't believe her ears. 'But we can't. It's a *crime scene,* isn't it?'

Vicky shrugged. 'Not as far as I know. The police haven't even been out here. They're obviously not taking all this ghost story stuff seriously.'

Emily gulped. She couldn't help feeling a little nervous about going into the haunted attic, but there might be crucial evidence in there. And how spooky could it be with three other people *and* in the middle of a bright sunny day, anyway? She had an investigation to get on with!

Vicky dropped her voice. 'Probably best if Mrs Bailey, the housekeeper, doesn't know about it, though. She's a bit of a battleaxe and we've been told not to let any reporters into the haunted room. But you're *not* reporters, are you? And they take people in that room on guided tours sometimes.' Vicky laughed. 'Just not after *midnight*, of course! We'd better leave Drift outside,' she added, smiling at the little dog who was happily munching on a stale custard cream. 'Dogs aren't really allowed in the manor and if Mrs Bailey sees him, we'll all be in for it.'

Emily tied Drift's lead to an iron boot-scraper on the doorstep, gave him a bowl of water and left him on Lookout Duty.

'Back in a minute,' she told him.

Nine

In Case of Emergency

Scott, Jack and Emily followed Vicky across the grand hall of the manor. Richly embroidered tapestries in reds and greens lined the walls between the old oak beams, and shafts of sunlight poured in through the latticed windows. The scent of beeswax polish mingled with that of old-fashioned roses arranged in huge vases on every chest and table. Scott smiled encouragingly at Emily. There was nothing spooky about this place.

It was just like any other historical building you got herded around on school trips.

'Meet Sarah Goodwell,' Vicky said, as if she was introducing a guest at a party.

Emily stopped in her tracks. Jack bumped into her.

'Could you signal if you're planning to do that again?' he joked.

Emily hardly heard him. 'Sarah Goodwell?' she stammered. *But that's impossible. Sarah Goodwell is the gho—*

Then she saw that Vicky was pointing up to an old oil painting on the wall, one of a collection of family portraits in ornate gilt frames.

'She wouldn't win any beauty contests, would she?' Scott laughed.

Emily took a deep breath and forced herself to look at Sarah Goodwell. Dark, beady eyes stared back from a pale, round face. Her thin lips were compressed into an expression halfway between a smile and a scowl. She wore a black dress with a low square neckline, and a purple birthmark covered her left cheek like a blackberry juice stain. A black cat with amber eyes was lying on her lap, almost invisible against the folds of her dress.

As they walked away Emily couldn't help turning back for another look. She could have sworn two pairs of eyes – one pair dark and beady, the other flecked with gold – were following her.

They were almost at the staircase when a door marked

MRS BAILEY, HOUSEKEEPER was opened by a middle-aged lady in a pale blue suit. Her silver hair was swept up in a bun and she wore a double string of pearls. 'Was there something you required, Victoria? I'm just popping out to check the film crew aren't trampling on the flower beds again,' she announced in a voice so posh that Scott thought for a moment she was doing an impression of the queen.

'Oh, no, nothing, Mrs Bailey,' Vicky mumbled.' I was just going to show my friends the, er, West Gallery.'

'School History project,' Emily piped up.

The housekeeper looked down her elegant nose. 'Yes, well, we do have some very *significant* paintings. Just keep sticky fingers well away!'

Vicky, Emily and Jack turned and began to climb the great curving oak staircase. Scott was about to follow them when he had an idea. 'I'll catch you up in a minute.' He patted the pockets of his shorts. 'Must have dropped my phone in the staff room.'

But it wasn't his phone he wanted to go back for. It was something he'd seen over Mrs Bailey's shoulder as she stood in the doorway of her office. The computer screen on the desk had been facing him, and on that screen was a spreadsheet. The contents were too small to read, of course, but the title had jumped out at him as if it was a flashing neon sign: CLEANING SHIFTS.

Scott stood outside Mrs Bailey's door. It wasn't his usual style to take mad risks that just invited Ten Types of Trouble. He usually left that kind of thing to Jack. But Mrs Bailey hadn't locked her office. All he had to do was open the door, take a few steps, and he would know which cleaners were on the night shift on Monday night and who might have seen Savannah Shaw near the haunted attic . . .

He couldn't actually believe that he was even *thinking* about doing this. But he could hear Jack's voice in his head: *Go on, don't be such a wimp, just do it!*

Mrs Bailey could be back from the garden at any moment. It was now or never.

Scott pushed open the door.

With his heart flailing around in his chest like a fish out of water, he ran his eyes over the computer screen. He found the column for Monday night, but the date was wrong. *Mrs Bailey must have been working on the rota for next week!* he realized. He didn't have time to start searching the computer files for the right spreadsheet now, so, annoyed and disappointed, he turned to leave. But as he did, he noticed a sheet of paper pinned to a corkboard. At first he thought it was the same as the spreadsheet on the screen, but then he saw the dates. It was *this* week's rota! He found the Monday night-shift and stared at the name, trying to burn it into his memory: Gabriella Moretti. Why couldn't it be something simple like Anne Smith?

Scott felt a wave of triumph. Mission accomplished! Emily and Jack were going to be so impressed. All he had to do now was make a speedy exit. He peeped round the door to check the coast was clear, but what he saw in the hall made him jump back as if he'd been electrocuted. Shaking from head to toe, he leant against the door. The triumph was gone. Mrs Bailey was standing at the bottom of the staircase, talking to Detective Inspector Hassan and a uniformed woman police officer.

Thoughts flew round Scott's head like a swarm of bees. *It's game over! I knew I shouldn't have listened to Jack! When was that ever a good idea? Why didn't I go up to the attic with the others? Any second now, the police will storm in and arrest me for trespassing, and I was only in here for a few seconds!*

A few seconds! That's when Scott realized: Mrs Bailey could hardly have dialled nine, nine, nine in the time he'd been in the office. There was no way the police could've driven from the station in Carrickstowe, across the causeway to the island, and along the coast road to Pendragon Manor in that time – even with blue lights and sirens. *They must be here about something else . . .* Scott took a deep breath, eased the door open a crack and peeped out again.

Scott had met Detective Inspector Hassan several times during Operation Treasure and, although he had his back turned, there was no mistaking the bear-like figure in the immaculate suit or the fringe of dark hair surrounding the bald patch that gleamed like the polished oak furniture in the hall. 'We need to seal off this so-called "haunted" room,' he boomed.

Mrs Bailey smiled serenely and raised her eyebrows a fraction.

'We've had a call from a member of the public,' the policewoman explained. 'We can't divulge the details but from this point in time we are treating it as a crime scene.'

Mrs Bailey ignored her and addressed Inspector Hassan in a business-like manner, as if mysterious incidents in haunted rooms were just another minor inconvenience in the life of a modern housekeeper – like reporters trampling flower beds and people leaving rings on the furniture with their coffee cups. 'I'll take you up there myself if you'll follow me.'

Scott watched them set off up the stairs. *What had happened in the haunted room?* Whatever it was, he had a feeling that it wasn't going to look good if Vicky, Emily and Jack were discovered by the police right in the middle of it. He had to warn them to get out of there. He grabbed his phone and called Emily, but she'd turned her phone off. Mrs Bailey and the police officers would reach the attic room at any moment. Scott crept out into the hall and looked around desperately for inspiration.

Then he found it. On the wall of the corridor that led to the kitchens sat a little red box, with a small metal hammer hanging below.

IN CASE OF EMERGENCY, BREAK GLASS.

Yep! This was *definitely* an emergency.

Ten

The Haunted Room

Meanwhile, Jack was following Vicky through a wall.

They'd climbed four sets of stairs, each one narrower, steeper and less grand than the last, to reach the attics, which must once have been the servants' quarters. Vicky had taken a key from a cleaners' cupboard on the second floor landing, and let them into a small room with a sloping ceiling. She walked over to the back wall, which was lined with wood panelling, thickly carved with a border of mythical beasts, and tugged on the outspread wing of a griffin. There was a creak and a click, and Vicky slid the entire panel to one side to reveal a low wooden door. 'Ta-da!'

'Wow!' Jack whistled. 'Cool or what?'

'Shouldn't we wait for Scott?' Emily was hanging back, looking nervously behind her.

'Nah,' Jack said. 'How long does it take him to find a phone anyway? I'm not waiting!'

He stepped into the room: bare wooden floorboards, plastered walls, a few cupboards. Motes of dust floating in the air were caught in a sunbeam shining through the small window. And this was supposed to be the secret laboratory of the Wicked Witch of the West. So where was the pentagram marked out on the floor? Where were the broomsticks, the cauldrons, the racks of newts' eyes and the shrunken heads? OK, maybe shrunken heads were more witch doctor than witch, but there was *nothing* creepy here at all! He'd been more scared than this playing *Snap*! He did a quick circuit of the room, glancing at display cabinets containing dusty old bottles and bits of pots. *Typical!* What was it with historians and bits of pots? There were some old books too. The label said GRIMOIRES but they looked like spellbooks. Those could be worth a look.

Hands in pockets, Jack wandered across to the window, ducking beneath the slope of the ceiling.

Through the thick swirly glass, he could see Brett diBlanco still holding forth to a group of reporters on the terrace. And there was that stalker guy with the goatee who'd been lurking in the maze. He was at it again, this time loitering near the parked cars on the drive . . . where a police car was now parked among the trailers and vans! *Interesting.* That hadn't been there before.

Jack turned back to the room. Vicky had opened a huge wardrobe with a mirrored door and was peering inside. Unfortunately it was empty and not stuffed with witches' hats and black cloaks. She closed it again.

'Come on, Em,' Jack called.

Emily put her head round the door. It was starting to dawn on Jack that she really was a bit scared of the whole haunted house thing. Weird! Usually Emily wasn't afraid of *anything*! Not like half the girls at school who screamed if they saw a spider (especially if they found one in a peanut butter sandwich in their lunchbox, not that *he* would know anything about that, of course!).

Jack took Emily by the arm and pulled her into the room. 'See. It's perfectly safe. Guaranteed one hundred per cent free of all known ghosts, witches and other paranormal household pests . . .'

Emily laughed. She stepped into the room and looked around. 'Yeah, you're right. It looks pretty normal in here. OK, let's start looking for clues.' Her voice suddenly broke off and she gaped at the wardrobe. 'W-w-what's that?'

'Er, that's what we scientists call your *reflection*!' Jack said. 'It's a *mirror*!' Honestly, Emily was getting a bit carried away with this whole ghost-phobia thing.

'No, not that. *That!*' Emily was pointing a trembling finger at the bottom of the wardrobe. Jack and Vicky both looked down. A note had been tucked into the mirror frame. It looked like some kind of parchment covered with old-fashioned writing in thick black ink.

'What is it?' Jack reached out to pick the note up.

'Don't touch!' Emily shouted. 'It could be cursed!' She paused. 'I mean, *poisoned,* or something.'

'Poisoned?' Jack echoed. 'It's probably just a shopping list!' But he snatched his hand away just in case. All this witchcraft mumbo-jumbo was starting to spook him too. *Was that a voice in the next room?* Now he was hearing things! No, someone was definitely walking around on the other side of the false wall. *Could it be the ghost?—*

Jack felt the hairs stand up on the back of his neck. Then he got a grip. *No, of course it isn't the ghost. It must be Scott finally back from the Great Phone Hunt,* he told himself. Jack was about to call out to his brother, when Emily clamped her hand over his mouth. 'Mmpph!' he mumbled. Now what was she doing?

Then he heard it. Someone was talking in the next room and it wasn't Scott. 'Oh, how *irritating*!' said the voice. 'Whoever came up here last has left the door wide open.'

Jack recognized the housekeeper's plummy accent. *Uh-oh! I bet we're going to get a rocket from Bossy Bailey for being in here.* He began to prepare his defence . . . *We were looking for the West Gallery and took a wrong turn . . .*

'Ah, yes, that must have been Mr Golding.' Jack recognised the new voice too. It was the big policeman with the mad moustache: D. I. Hassan. What was *he* doing here? Maybe they were in a shedload more trouble than he thought . . .

'Sid Golding phoned us and reported that he'd come across some kind of ransom note in the haunted room this morning,' Detective Inspector Hassan was saying. 'Probably a silly prank of some sort, but if it *does* contain a threat to Savannah Shaw's safety, we'll be treating it *very seriously indeed*. After you, Mrs Bailey.'

Jack was in full panic-stations mode now. *We're going to get blamed for this note,* he thought. *We'll be arrested for Savannah Shaw's kidnapping . . .* Suddenly he felt someone grab his elbow. *The long arm of the law! No, hang on, it's Vicky . . . What's she doing?*

Next thing he knew, Jack was inside the wardrobe, wedged between Vicky and Emily, his nose pressed up against the back of the door. He wasn't sure that being trapped in the wardrobe was actually a radical improvement on the situation. Any faint hope of getting away with a 'wrong-turn' excuse was definitely out of the window now. He remembered that book where some kids found a magical portal in the back of an old wardrobe that led into the snow-covered world of Narnia. *Was that too much to ask for?* He felt behind him. *Solid wood: one. Magical portals: nil.*

'This'll be the note, then,' Inspector Hassan's voice came from millimetres away on the other side of the wardrobe door.

The air in the wardrobe was full of a suffocating chloriney pong. Jack had never smelled mothballs before but he guessed he was getting a lungful now. For the first time in his life, he felt sorry for moths.

His nose tickled. Suddenly he had an irresistible urge to sneeze.

'Ah-chooooo!'

Eleven

The Mysterious Message

I t was a very loud sneeze.

But at the very same instant – and just as Emily was bracing herself for Inspector Hassan to throw open the door and ask what *precisely* they thought they were doing inside the wardrobe – another noise drowned it out.

The fire alarm!

Emily couldn't believe their luck.

'Are you expecting a fire drill this morning, Mrs Bailey?' D. I. Hassan's voice pulsed with impatience.

'No, certainly not. We must follow the correct evacuation procedure immediately!'

'Some idiot burning toast in the kitchens, no doubt,' D. I. Hassan grumbled. 'Alright, we're coming. We'll bag this note and take it with us. Don't want our evidence burning to a crisp, do we?'

Emily waited for their footsteps to die away, took a deep breath and then tumbled out of the wardrobe. At least the prospect of being caught by the police had taken her mind off being caught by the ghost.

Vicky was making for the door already. 'Phew! I didn't fancy being dragged off to the police station again! I've only just got over my last visit. Let's get out of here,' she said. 'We'll go down the back stairs. No one will notice us in all the confusion.'

Luckily, in her haste to follow the *correct evacuation procedure*, Mrs Bailey had forgotten to slide the wooden panel back into place, and only a few minutes later Emily was running along the kitchen corridor towards the back door. There wasn't even a hint of smoke. The fire seemed to have been a false alarm, but Emily was worried about Drift. She hadn't told him she'd be gone so long . . .

'Drift!' she called. 'I'm back.'

But the little dog was nowhere to be seen. The bowl of water was still there. The iron boot-scraper was still there. But Drift and his lead had vanished.

Emily's heart went into freefall. *Someone's taken him!* She felt Jack gripping her by both elbows.

'Don't worry, we'll find him,' he said firmly.

Emily couldn't bear it if anything had happened to Drift.

'Pssst! Over here!' The voice seemed to be coming from a row of runner beans twining their way up wigwams of poles in the vegetable garden.

Suddenly Jack was laughing. 'It's Scott! He's behind those beans. And he's got Drift.'

Emily ran round the end of the beanpoles and threw her arms around Drift. 'Thank goodness you're OK!' she sobbed. Drift wriggled happily and licked her face. Emily was so relieved she could have kissed Scott *and* Jack. But then she thought better of it and kissed Drift instead. There were some things a girl would never live down!

⌒

By the time they'd cycled back to Stone Cottage, the friends were hot, tired and hungry. They flopped down in the long grass in the back garden and fell upon the tray of sandwiches and lemonade that Aunt Kate brought out for them like a flock of ravenous vultures. It was only after his second round of cheese and tomato that Jack was strong enough to re-engage non-essential functions

– like winding Scott up. 'You missed *everything*, mate. The haunted room was *awesome*, dead spooky! Then there was this mega police *raid . . .*'

Scott rolled his eyes so far they were in danger of going into orbit. 'Yeah, I did sort of *notice* the police . . .'

Emily broke off from feeding Drift pieces of ham and shot Scott a suspicious look. 'It was *you* who set off the fire alarm, wasn't it?'

Scott laughed. 'Guilty as charged!'

'Lucky you went back for your phone,' Emily said.

'Yeah, about that . . . ' Scott explained his foray into Mrs Bailey's office. 'Monday's night-shift cleaner was on the rota. It's someone called Gabriella Moretti!' He stretched back on the grass, fingers laced behind his head.

'Wow! Great work!' Emily took out her notebook and began to write. 'We should be able to trace her now we have a name . . .'

Jack stared at his brother. Scott didn't usually go in for heroic solo missions. 'Yeah, give the boy a biscuit!' he joked, but he couldn't help feeling a tiny flicker of respect for his older brother. Respect mixed with jealousy. *Why didn't I think of raiding Bossy Bailey's office?* 'Yeah, well, *we* found a *ransom* note,' he said, trying to play the trump card.

Scott sat up. 'Wow! What did it say?'

Jack sighed. 'That's the thing. Old Hassan turned up

before we had time to read it. And he took it away with him!'

'Well, that's *really* useful!' Scott groaned. 'What's the use of a ransom note if we have no way of knowing what it says?'

'Ah, but we *do*!' At that moment, Emily sounded like some kind of fairy godmother to Jack, but instead of pulling out a wand and turning pumpkins into coaches, she pulled her phone out of her bag. 'I was just taking a photo when we heard the police . . . I think I got it . . . Yes, here it is . . . '

Scott took one look, then howled with laughter. 'You've caught Jack in the mirror, Em. His hair's sticking up on end! This is another classic for Facebook . . . '

Jack punched Scott's arm and grabbed the phone. He had to admit, he did look pretty hilarious, but he *was* being bundled into a wardrobe at the time! He peered at the photo. 'The note's really small and blurry. I can't read a word.'

'Yeah, well, I didn't have a lot of time to line up the perfect shot . . . ' Emily said.

'We might be able to see it on a bigger screen.' Scott jumped up and ran into the kitchen.

Aunt Kate was busy baking apple pies, so she didn't mind the friends borrowing the computer she used for writing her novels. Scott jiggled the mouse and raised his eyebrows as he noticed the webpage Aunt Kate had left open. '*Safe-breaking for Beginners*? Perhaps she has a secret life as a bank robber!'

Emily grinned. 'That could be our *next* investigation . . .'

Scott uploaded the photo from Emily's phone, zoomed in on the note and increased the contrast to make the writing clearer. At least, that was the theory. They could *see* the writing now, but they still couldn't make sense of it.

Jack sighed. 'It must be Arabic or Double Dutch or something. It's all upside-down and back-to-front.'

'Back to front! That's it!' Emily shouted. 'You're a *genius*, Jack!'

Jack tried to look as if he knew what she was talking about. 'Yeah, well, you know, I'm just naturally gifted . . .'

Emily squinted at the screen with her head on one side. 'I need a mirror!'

Girls! Jack thought as he fetched a mirror from the bathroom. *What's she going to do? Check her hair?*

But when Jack handed her the mirror Emily held it up to the computer screen and angled it so that it reflected the writing. It was still difficult to read because the script was some ancient style with curlicues and flourishes, but at last the squiggles had turned into real letters . . .

Scott read the message out loud.

She who has entered my chamber past the midnight hour will remain locked in darkness. Only her true love can lift the curse. S. G.

Emily's hand shook so much she almost dropped the mirror. 'It's signed with Sarah Goodwell's initials.'

'Ooh, what fun! Mirror writing?' Aunt Kate leaned over Emily's shoulder, and nearly made her jump out of her chair. She wiped her floury hands on her apron. 'Mmmm, interesting. Leonardo da Vinci was famous for using mirror writing, you know.'

Scott had no idea who had kidnapped Savannah, but he was pretty sure it wasn't Leonardo da Vinci! 'Emily's been telling us about some of the local legends,' he explained, trying not to give too much away. Aunt Kate generally let the boys get on with their own thing, but even *she* might object to them getting mixed up with what was starting to look like a full-blown kidnapping case.

'Did I hear you say *Sarah Goodwell*, Emily?' Aunt Kate asked. 'I did a bit of research into that old Midnight Ghost legend a couple of years ago for a book I was writing. Before she was accused of being a witch, everyone on the island used to go to her for herbal remedies and love potions. She was a matchmaker more than anything else. When they turned against her, people started saying her birthmark was "the devil's mark" and that her pet cat was her "familiar".'

'Bit like Emily and Drift, then!' Jack joked. But

Emily was still so shaken by the message that she didn't even have the energy to object.

Aunt Kate perched her glasses on her nose and peered at the message in the mirror. 'But this note wasn't written by Sarah Goodwell – or anyone from the sixteenth century for that matter! Someone's been very clever, copying Tudor-style letters and using mirror-writing to make it all seem a bit more mystical, but they've made some mistakes. In those days, people used the long letter "s" – you know, the one that looks like an f – except at the end of a word. And the spelling of the words is far too modern too. Sorry to spoil your fun, kids.'

Emily grinned. This was the best news she'd heard all day: no ghosts, no witches, no spooky stuff at all! Just an ordinary threatening note, written by an ordinary flesh-and-blood criminal.

Now, *this* was the kind of mystery she could handle!

Twelve

Searching for Clues

Operation Lost Star kept Scott, Jack and Emily busy for the rest of the afternoon and most of the following day.

Their first task was to track down Gabriella Moretti. If she'd spotted Savannah in the manor on Monday night, it was possible that she'd seen the kidnapper as well without even realizing it. They had to talk to her.

Scott fetched Aunt Kate's telephone directory

and they phoned all the Morettis in Cornwall. There weren't many. But none of them knew of anyone called Gabriella. Next, Emily phoned every cleaning agency in the Carrickstowe area and asked if they employed a Gabriella Moretti. 'She's won a competition,' she recited, crossing her fingers firmly each time, 'and may be entitled to claim a prize.' They were about to give up when the secretary at the sixth agency recognized the name and confirmed that Gabriella worked there. She even gave Emily a phone number, but it turned out to be a youth hostel and Gabriella had checked out weeks ago.

Scott sighed. They'd reached a dead end. His daring mission into Mrs Bailey's office had all been for nothing.

＿

The friends met at the oak tree for a planning meeting next morning. Emily wrote a new heading in her notebook: *Suspects.* 'First, Sid Golding,' she said. 'He supposedly *found* the note and reported it to the police. But he could easily have planted it there himself.'

'Yeah, but why would he kidnap Savannah?' Scott asked. 'He's the one who's so worried about anything happening to her.'

Emily chewed her pencil. 'You're right. We'd have to establish a motive.'

'What if someone's trying to *frame* Golding?' Jack

asked. 'Someone who's got a grudge against him.'

'Like Max Fordham?' Scott suggested.

Emily and Jack stared at him in horror. 'I'm not saying Max *did* it!' Scott laughed. 'I think he's great too. But he's not exactly in the Sid Golding Appreciation Society, is he? *Sleazy,* I think was the word he used.'

'OK,' Emily admitted reluctantly. 'We'll add him to the list of suspects. And Lauren O'Brien? She has to do all the dangerous stunts while Savannah gets the fame and glory. Maybe she's jealous?'

'What about Brett diBlanco?' Scott suggested. 'He came out of the manor just after Golding yesterday. He could have been up in the attic planting the note. Although, why would he kidnap his own girlfriend?'

'Let's face it, it could have been anyone!' Jack said. 'One of the film crew or the other actors. Or someone working at the manor. I can definitely see Bossy Bailey as a kidnapper. *We have to follow the correct kidnapping procedure!*' Jack mimicked the housekeeper's posh voice. 'And what about that guy with the goatee we saw hanging around? Obsessed Stalker or Innocent Bystander? Or it could've been Sarah Goodwell, of course!' *In most cases,* Jack thought, *having been dead for the last four hundred years would be a rock solid alibi, but in this investigation, nothing is quite that simple!*

There was a long silence as the three friends

contemplated how little they had to go on. 'We're officially *clueless*!' Emily sighed.

Jack watched Emily doodling patterns around the names in her notebook. She'd drawn a little heart above *Max Fordham*. He decided not to mention it. Last time he teased Emily when they were sitting in the tree, he'd ended up head-planting into a pile of acorns. He noticed that Emily had stuck a copy of the ghost-note into her notebook; Scott had photographed the reflected message in the mirror and printed it out. Jack gazed at the message . . . There was something nagging at the back of his mind . . . The note reminded him of being in History Class at school – which was weird. They did a lot of things in History that Jack considered random, but faking notes from ghosts in mirror writing hadn't been one of them so far! He pictured himself in Double History, trying to stay awake, copying Ruby McEllery's notes . . . Then it came to him! Ruby wrote the dots over her "i"s as little circles. Sometimes she even made them into little smiley faces or love hearts. *That was it!*

'You've been staring at that note for ages,' Scott laughed. 'Have you discovered the meaning of life yet?'

'Nah, it's just that the dots over all the "i"s are circles,' Jack replied.

Emily took a look. 'Oh yeah. Maybe it was fashionable to write like that in Tudor times?'

Scott shook his head. 'No. I looked up some websites

on sixteenth century scripts last night to find out about those long letter "s"s that Aunt Kate told us about. There was nothing about circles.'

'And there's no reason to do circles just because it's mirror writing,' Emily's voice flickered with excitement. 'A dot is a dot whichever way you look at it. And that means that whoever wrote this note probably *always* dots their "i"s with a circle!'

Scott punched the air. 'Houston, we have a clue!'

'I've just been a total genius again, haven't I?' Jack said with a grin. 'I'm on a roll here. I think I'll apply to go on University Challenge!'

Emily snapped her notebook shut. 'Right. We need to get writing samples from all the suspects and see which ones dot their "i"s with little circles.'

Scott wasn't convinced. 'We can't just pole up to people and say *Excuse me, would you mind writing a few words for me? Preferably ones with lots of "i"s in them?*'

'Like *invisibility*,' Jack said. 'That's got five!'

Emily jumped down from the branch. 'Of course not. We'll buy a couple of fancy notebooks from the newsagents and pretend we're collecting autographs.'

'Good idea! What if they don't have an "i" in their name though?' Jack asked.

Scott thought for a moment. 'I know! We'll pretend the autograph book is a present for Emily's birthday. If they have to write *Happy Birthday, Emily,* they'll have to dot two "i"s . . . '

Emily smiled. 'It's not exactly my ideal birthday present, but it should work!'

—

They decided to split up to cover more ground.

Jack, Emily and Drift headed up to the castle and asked Max Fordham and Lauren O'Brien for their autographs. Max and Lauren were both delighted to help, but neither wrote their dots as circles.

'If you want to hang around for a while you can watch the helicopter sequence,' Max called, as he abseiled over the cliff edge, roped together with Lauren. 'Just keep behind that barrier over there. In fact, here comes the chopper now!'

The beating of the rotors was growing louder and louder. Jack looked at Emily. They really *should* go to Pendragon Manor and help Scott, *but this was people leaping off cliffs onto helicopters!*

Emily grinned. 'I'm sure Scott can manage without us. And it'd be rude not to stay after Max invited us!'

—

Collecting autographs in a pink *Hello Kitty* notebook was probably the most toe-curlingly uncool thing Scott had ever done in his life. 'I'm collecting them as a birthday present for my friend, Emily,' he recited, ambushing everyone he encountered at Pendragon Manor. 'She's totally *obsessed* with Agent Diamond films!' he said, to explain why he wanted the autographs, not only of all the actors, but also of the assistant wardrobe manager and the third cameraman.

Everyone wrote in his book. Everyone, that was, apart from Brett diBlanco. 'Sorry, kid,' he said, looking up from his sun-lounger, with a lazy smile that was anything *but* sorry, 'but if I gave out autographs to *every* star-struck admirer, I'd never do anything else! You can send off to the address on my website and my agent will deal with it.'

Scott was tempted to point out that signing the autograph would have taken considerably less of Brett's oh-so-valuable time than explaining why he *wasn't* going to sign it, but at that moment he spotted the skinny guy with the goatee hovering behind a coffee kiosk that had been set up near the maze. *Who is he? And why is he hanging around the set? Only one way to find out,* Scott thought, hurrying over, waving his autograph book.

The man laughed. 'Sorry. I'm not with the Agent Diamond crew. I'm just a gatecrasher.'

'Gatecrasher?' Scott asked.

The man fished a photo-ID card out of his jeans pocket and held it up. 'Neil Denton. Journalist with *The Carrickstowe Times*.'

Scott grinned. 'So, you're *not* a psychotically obsessed fan then?'

Neil Denton shook his head. 'I'm working on an investigative piece about Golding. There are rumours that he's been putting some of his millions into some very dodgy business deals, maybe even with links to organized crime. So, as you can imagine, I'm not exactly Mr Popular with him . . . '

'So *that's* why you were lurking in the maze the other day?' Scott asked.

'Yeah! Golding threatened to sue me if he caught me on set again!'

Scott laughed. 'Yeah, I know that feeling.'

'Talk of the devil, here he is now . . .'

Sid Golding's Ferrari was pulling into the car park.

Scott couldn't believe his luck. He had thirty-two autographs in his book, and, so far, there was not a single circle over a single "i". Surely that was all about to change. Sid Golding was the prime suspect, and now was Scott's chance to *prove* he'd written the ghost-note. He turned to say goodbye to Neil Denton, but the journalist had already melted away. Scott grabbed a double-shot espresso from the coffee stand, dashed across the lawn, and whipped open the door of the Ferrari before Golding had even turned off the engine. Scott held up the coffee. 'Double-shot espresso, sir?'

But, as Golding reached out, Scott snatched the

coffee away and thrust the pen into his hand instead. 'Autograph, please!'

Caught by surprise, Golding took the pen and scrawled his name across the blank page Scott was holding open for him. Then he came to his senses. Shoving the book back at Scott, he clutched the top of the car door and began hauling himself out of the driver's seat. 'Out of my way! *Someone!* Who let these damned autograph hunters in here?'

Scott handed over the coffee and stepped back from the car. Trembling with anticipation, he looked down at the page.

Sid Golding. Both of the "i"s were dotted with . . . *dots.*

Thirteen

The Manor at Midnight

That night an event was taking place on the island that rivalled even Agent Diamond for excitement. A huge meteor shower was due to be visible from ten o'clock and the residents of Castle Key had organized a party on Westward Beach on the western tip of the island to view the spectacle. Mr and Mrs Wild had to stay at The Lighthouse to look after their guests, and Aunt Kate said she had too much work to do (although

Jack suspected she was planning to spend the evening out robbing banks), but they agreed that Emily and the boys could go by themselves and camp on the beach; they would be quite safe with so many of their friends and neighbours from the village close by.

The friends set out early in the evening with their tents strapped to the back of their bikes: a heavy canvas construction from Aunt Kate's shed for the boys – so ancient that Scott suspected it had last been occupied by some Victorian explorer searching for the source of the Zambezi River – and a modern pop-up tent for Emily and Drift. They also had backpacks full of picnic food and provisions for a campfire breakfast. It was a warm, cloudless evening and Scott, Jack and Emily – with Drift in his bike basket, of course – were brimming with excitement as they joined the throngs of people making their way along the country road over the moor to Westward Beach.

It was good to take a break from Operation Lost Star, Emily thought. Their investigations had ground to a halt; their obsessed fan had turned out to be a reporter, none of the autographs they'd collected had matched the note from the haunted attic and the hunt for Gabriella Moretti had gone nowhere. They badly needed a new lead.

They found a perfect spot to pitch the tents in the shelter of a sand dune. Then there was swimming and body-boarding in the surf before settling down to eat their picnic. Families and groups of friends were lighting barbecues and playing volleyball and French cricket. The beat from a reggae band accompanied the gentle crashing of the waves. Scott joined in a massive game of football, then borrowed a guitar and jammed with the band.

'Ah, bliss!' Jack sighed, lying back on the rug to watch the meteor shower. At first, all he could see was a standard-issue black velvet sky with a few stars strewn about like silver glitter. 'OK, you can start the show now, in your own time . . .' he said.

Suddenly Scott shouted 'There!' A star was zooming down towards the sea. And then another and another!

Emily made wishes on the shooting stars but there were so many that she ran out of things to wish for. She started making wishes for Drift, but it seemed his dreams had already come true, as he gnawed enthusiastically at a pork chop he'd pilfered from a nearby barbecue.

'I've had a thought . . .' Scott said, as the meteor shower finally dwindled to the last few sparks. 'We're only five minutes from Pendragon Manor. We could go and see if any of the cleaners are there. Even if Gabriella's not at work, one of the others might know how we could find her . . .'

'Cool,' Jack was already on his feet. 'I fancy a midnight bike ride!'

Emily hesitated. Her stomach did a rollercoaster-lurch. Pendragon Manor was creepy enough during the daytime. At night it was going to be like something out of a nightmare. Sarah Goodwell *was* called the *Midnight Ghost*, after all. But Scott was right. The chance to locate Gabriella Moretti was too good to miss. *A professional agent never lets fear cloud her judgment,* Emily told herself. *You wouldn't see Maya Diamond acting like a big drip just because of a stupid old ghost story!*

She flicked on her bike lights and Drift jumped into his basket. 'Let's go!'

It wasn't too bad cycling along the lane, lit only by their bike lights and a sliver of moon. But as the silhouette of the manor came into view, the dark woods seemed to close in around them. Unseen owls hooted from the treetops. 'It's OK, Drift,' Emily whispered, as she followed Jack and Scott's red tail lights into the drive. 'There's *nothing* to be frightened of.'

A white van inscribed with the logo Clean Sweep was parked near the gate to the manor. The driver was fast asleep inside, his feet up on the dashboard.

'Result!' Scott breathed. 'The cleaners are here.'

They propped their bikes up against the wall and crept through the gardens. Halfway across the lawn Emily stopped behind the yew maze and glanced up at the house. Light spilled out from windows at one end of the ground floor. It looked as if the cleaners were working in the kitchens. The rest of the building was in darkness, apart from the security lights long the roof-line, which cast grotesque shadows of the gargoyles –

winged demons, hideous beasts and horned monsters – across the walls.

'That one looks a bit like Scott!' Jack whispered. Then he screamed and began swatting the air. 'Aggh! What was that?'

Emily jumped. Black shapes flitted in front of her eyes and brushed her face. 'They're just bats!' she laughed.

'Just bats?' Jack groaned. 'I practically had a heart attack!'

'They won't hurt you,' Emily said. 'They're always around on summer nights.' Emily wasn't scared of a few *bats*! But she *was* scared of seeing that ghostly figure at the attic window again. She didn't want to look, but somehow her eyes were drawn to the small diamond-paned windows under the roof.

Suddenly she saw it! A flicker of light behind the dark glass.

Emily grabbed hold of Scott's arm. 'Did you see it?' she breathed.

Scott looked around. 'See what?'

Jack pointed. 'Yeah, I saw it. A light!'

'Is . . . that . . . the . . . ?' Emily stammered.

'The haunted room? Yes,' Jack said. 'I looked out of that window when we were up there and it's in line with that pine tree.'

The three friends stared at the window. The light gleamed again: a small, restless glimmer, as if from a candle or a lantern. Someone was moving about up there.

Surely, the cleaners don't clean the attic rooms? Scott thought. He checked his watch. It was half past eleven. Too early for the Midnight Ghost. *Not that ghosts exist, of course*, he reminded himself. Although somehow it was harder to be *quite* so sure, what with the owls and the bats and the gargoyle-shadows and the glimmering light.

'It's probably the kidnapper leaving another note,' Jack whispered.

'What if it's *Savannah* up there?' Emily asked in a tiny voice. 'The note said she was locked in darkness.' She tried to ignore it, but the little voice at the back of her mind wouldn't go away. *What if it's the ghost of Sarah Goodwell?* it said.

'Let's go and check it out!' Jack set off towards the house. If Savannah Shaw was imprisoned in the attic, it would be so cool. He'd be like a knight in shining armour rescuing the damsel in distress. Well, OK, scratch the armour, his BMX helmet and kneepads would do . . . Shame there were no dragons around to polish off on the way . . . He turned and realized that Scott and Emily weren't following him.

'No way!' Emily was saying. 'We can't go in there. It's almost midnight.'

'There's no ghost,' Scott said. 'You heard Aunt Kate. That note was a fake.'

Emily shook her head. 'It's alright for you two. Sarah Goodwell's curse doesn't affect *boys*.'

'That's sex discrimination,' Jack laughed. 'Hasn't she heard of equal opportunities?'

'Not helping!' Emily snapped.

'You could stay here with Drift and wait for us?' Scott offered.

More than anything in the world, Emily longed to jump on her bike and pedal as fast as her legs would carry her back to the beach. But there was no way she was going to let the boys do this without her. No way she was going to let them know how bone-crushingly *petrified* she really was . . .

'I'm coming,' she said.

———

Luckily the cleaners had left the back door unlocked. Scott could hear a tap running in the kitchen and a radio tuned to a late-night phone-in.

'Let's go up to the attic and see what's going on there first,' he whispered. 'We'll stop by the kitchens and see if Gabriella is here on our way out.'

They crept across the hall. Sarah Goodwell's pale face glowed a ghoulish green in the light of an EXIT sign over the front door. Two dark eyes and two bright amber eyes bored down from the painting. Cold fingers of fear wrapped themselves around Emily's throat as she tried not to look back. Sensing her terror, Drift stuck close to her side, his ears back and his tail tucked between his legs. Emily forced herself to put one foot in front of the other and climb the stairs. Now, all that mattered was not letting the boys out of her sight.

By the second-floor landing it was pitch dark. Emily pulled a small torch from her bag, shone it into the cleaners' cupboard and found the key for the haunted room – just as she had seen Vicky White do on their first visit. But when they reached the room next to the haunted attic, the door wasn't locked. Scott entered and beckoned for the others to follow. They paused inside the door, ears straining for a sound. There was no one there. Scott shone the torch into the dark interior. The carved panel had been pulled back and the door was open. Little by little, they inched forwards. A floorboard creaked beneath Jack's foot and they all froze. Emily thought her heart would leap out of her mouth. But nothing happened. They went on. At last they were standing on the threshold of the haunted room.

Hardly daring to look, Emily followed Scott and Jack inside. One of the display cases had been opened and a huge leather-bound spellbook was lying open on the floor. White circles and pentacles had been daubed on the walls.

'Those weren't here before,' Jack whispered. His voice trembled and his face was white in the torchlight.

Gripped by terror, Emily stared at the symbols on the walls. *The legend was true!* Sarah Goodwell really *was* a witch and her ghost was back for revenge. She was here somewhere, right now, performing her terrible rituals. The spellbooks, the symbols, it all made sense. Sarah Goodwell had cursed Savannah and made her vanish and now she was waiting for another victim to lock in darkness . . . *And it was almost midnight!* Emily knew that she had to get out of that room before . . .

Drift's ears pricked up. The floorboard in the outer room creaked. Someone was coming.

Emily's knees buckled beneath her. *This was it!* She felt a cold hand grab her from behind. She just had time to reach for Drift's collar.

Somewhere in the house, a clock struck twelve.

Fourteen

A Surprise Discovery

When Emily opened her eyes, she was in darkness. The smell of mothballs and old wood was familiar. *She was inside the wardrobe!* And she was not alone. There was someone else squeezed in next to her. Dreading who – or what – she would see, she shone her torch around. Thankfully there was no pale round face with beady black eyes and a birthmark on her cheek. And there was no black cat with burning amber eyes.

She recognized a white t-shirt and a shock of blond hair.

It was Jack and Scott who'd pulled her into the wardrobe. The relief was overwhelming. Her heart still galloping like a runaway horse, Emily felt like crying, or laughing, or both, but she knew she had to stay calm. She closed her eyes and took a deep breath.

'You OK, Em?' Jack whispered. 'Sorry I grabbed you so hard.'

'Shh!' Scott hissed. 'And turn the torch off. The light might show around the door.'

Emily put her eye to the narrow gap between the hinges and made out a figure in a hooded black cloak enter the room. The figure knelt and held up a small lantern. In the pool of tawny light, a hand reached out and placed a scroll of paper inside the spellbook on the floor. Emily tried to look away but she was transfixed by fear. The figure turned, but the face was hidden beneath the folds of the black hood.

Suddenly Emily felt Drift scrabbling with his paws behind her. 'Drift, stop it!' she whispered.

But the little dog was making growling noises in his throat as if he was playing tug of war. Terrified they'd be heard, Emily looked out through the crack again. The figure was moving away. But suddenly it paused and held the lantern higher. It turned and looked at the wardrobe. Any second now it would open the door . . . Emily clutched Scott's arm.

At the same moment, Scott felt Jack – whose face had been pressed between his shoulder blades – lurch backwards. Scott turned to catch him, but Jack wasn't there. Scott put out his hands and felt around. His mind was a whirlpool of confusion. The space that, seconds ago, had been filled with his noisy, solid twelve-year-old brother, was now totally empty. He took the torch from Emily and, shielding the light as best he could so it wouldn't show through the gap in the door, he shone it behind him. The back of the wardrobe had disappeared! Drift was sitting in the corner with his jaws clamped firmly round a small wooden lever sticking up from the floor of the wardrobe. Behind him, Jack was lying flat on his back in what seemed to be another small attic.

In a single movement, Scott pushed Drift and Emily into the newly-discovered room. 'Come on, let's get out of here!'

They stumbled forwards, Emily's torch-beam swinging across rough plastered walls and rafters.

'Look!' Jack hissed, scrambling to his feet. 'There's a door!'

The door in the wood panelling under the slope of the ceiling was only waist-height but it was the only one Scott could see. He threw himself at it and pulled it open. As he crawled in behind Emily, Jack and Drift, the chamber behind him was flooded with lantern-light. Scott glanced back to see a black figure stepping through from the false back of the wardrobe. He didn't wait to see any more.

Blindly, the friends scurried like mice along the roof-space under the eaves. After a few minutes, Scott stopped to listen. There was no sound other than the faint scratching of real rodents. Either the black figure hadn't seen them or had decided not to follow them. They crawled through the warren of passages and ducts for what seemed like days. At last they reached a small door and pushed it open.

'I know where we are now,' Emily whispered. 'We've come through into the back of the cleaners' cupboard.'

They clambered over brooms and mops and polishing machines and opened the door onto the landing. There was no one around. Without a word, the three friends and Drift ran down the stairs, out of the back door and across the lawn to their bikes.

They didn't stop pedalling until they reached their tents at the beach.

＊

When Jack woke up, he wasn't sure where he was. Then he felt the nylon of his sleeping bag and smelled warm sun on canvas.

He'd had the weirdest dream last night! *They'd gone into the haunted room and he'd fallen through the back of the wardrobe . . .* Then he stretched and he felt the bruises on his back and his knees and it started to come back to him . . . *It wasn't a dream!* They really *did* see the ghost, or at least Emily did, through the crack in the wardrobe door. She'd told them about the black-hooded figure when they were safely back at the beach last night, sitting round their campfire boiling water for hot chocolate. And Scott said he'd seen the figure too as they crawled into the roof-space. Jack hadn't seen *anything* apart from the back of Scott's t-shirt in the wardrobe, and mouse-droppings under the eaves. It was *so* unfair!

Scott was still snoring in his sleeping bag. Jack began to doze off again. He was woken by a voice. The family in the next tent was making breakfast, and had switched on the radio. *'It's eight o'clock and here is the news . . . '* Jack zoned out as the newsreader droned on about house prices and budget cuts, but suddenly he caught some words that made him open his eyes and sit bolt upright.

' . . . a new twist in the bizarre disappearance of film star Savannah Shaw on the remote Cornish island of Castle Key . . . '

Jack held his breath. *' . . . publicity agent, Sid Golding, claims this morning to have found a second note in the haunted room in Pendragon Manor where Savannah Shaw has allegedly been abducted by the ghost of a sixteenth-century witch . . . '*

Scott rolled over. 'Ughh, what time is it?'

'Shhhh!' Jack hissed.

' . . . this latest note, apparently written by Savannah Shaw herself, is reported to confirm that she is trapped inside the haunted room, and can only be released from the curse that holds her there by her true love . . . ' There

was a wobble in the newsreader's voice that hinted he was not taking the story entirely seriously.

Emily was still half asleep when the boys crashed into her tent.

Drift leapt up from his position curled comfortably round her knees and welcomed them with a wagging tail. Emily was less enthusiastic. She sat up and pulled on a jumper and tried to make sense of what Scott and Jack were on about. Something about the radio and Sid Golding and a note from Savannah Shaw . . .

'Slow down,' she laughed. 'Let me get my head round this!'

To her surprise, Emily was feeling *fantastic* this morning, considering how close she'd come to keeling over and dying of fright in the haunted attic last night. Not only had she proved the legend wrong by being there past midnight and surviving to tell the tale, but she also knew that the sinister black-hooded figure they'd seen was *not* the ghost of Sarah Goodwell – or of anyone else for that matter.

It was a very *alive* human being, up to no good, in a long black cloak.

The question was, *which* human being? It was too tall to be Sid Golding. Savannah was tall, of course. But Emily was sure it was a man . . . unless . . . 'Did you notice anything unusual about Savannah Shaw's feet when we met her?' Emily asked.

The boys looked at each other. They clearly thought

the nocturnal encounter in the haunted room had driven their friend slightly mad.

'You mean like webbed feet or six toes or something?' Jack asked.

Scott grinned. 'Well, I did notice she was wearing these really slinky black high-heeled boots . . .'

'So, you didn't think her feet were particularly *big* then?'

The boys shook their heads.

'The person we saw in the haunted room last night had huge feet. Like size twelve or something. And he was wearing trainers! I caught a glimpse of them under the cloak when I peeped out from the wardrobe. That's when I knew for sure it wasn't Sarah Goodwell.'

Jack laughed. 'Trainers weren't really a fashion trend in the sixteenth century. But, if our Midnight Ghost wasn't Sarah Goodwell, and it wasn't Sid Golding or Savannah Shaw, who was it?'

'Brett diBlanco?' Scott suggested. 'He's the only one we haven't ruled out for the first note because he was too mean to sign an autograph. And he's pretty tall.'

'*And* he's a creep!' Jack pointed out.

Emily had an idea. 'What if Sid Golding and Brett diBlanco are a double-act? DiBlanco plants the notes and Golding 'finds' them. They could be staging the whole thing just to get extra publicity for the new Agent Diamond film.'

Scott nodded. 'Golding would do anything to

create more media interest . . .' Then he remembered his conversation with the reporter, Neil Denton. 'And maybe he wants a really big story to shift everyone's attention away from his own dubious financial dealings!'

As they cooked bacon and eggs for breakfast over the campfire, Emily couldn't stop wondering about Savannah. If Golding and diBlanco had faked the kidnapping, they must be keeping her hidden away somewhere. But she'd been gone three days now. That was a long time to be kept prisoner, even if she wasn't actually in grave danger. At last she came to a decision. 'We have to tell the police what we saw last night.'

The boys nodded. 'Even though we'll probably be grounded for life for going into the manor in the middle of the night,' Jack groaned.

Emily pulled out her mobile, called Carrickstowe Police Station, and asked for Detective Inspector Hassan.

'He's just been called out to an Emergency Press Conference,' the receptionist replied.

'Would that be at Pendragon Manor?' Emily asked politely.

'Sorry, I can't give out that information.'

But from the slight hesitation in the receptionist's voice, Emily knew she was right. Emergency Press Conference! There must have been a major development in the case. There was no time to lose.

'Quick, let's get the tents packed up,' she shouted to the boys. 'We've got a press conference to go to!'

Fifteen

The Press Conference

When Scott, Jack and Emily arrived at Pendragon Manor, it was even busier than on the first day of filming. There were three police cars in the drive, as well as a flock of outside broadcasting vehicles from various TV and radio stations. It seemed the press conference was major news.

The friends were taking a short cut across the vegetable garden, hoping to sneak in through the back door and find out what was going on, when Drift stopped between two rows of raspberry canes. His ears flicked up into Listening Formation. Emily motioned for Jack and Scott to halt.

They followed Drift's ears towards a stand of gooseberry bushes to find a woman sitting, slumped over, her head on her knees. Long dark hair spilled down across her shins. Drift trotted over and nuzzled his head against her arm.

Emily couldn't believe her eyes. *Was it really . . .*

'*Savannah?*' Jack gasped.

But the eyes that looked up were not emerald green. They were deep brown. They were also red-rimmed and smudged with dark rings. Emily knelt down and gave the woman a tissue from her bag. She took it and wiped her nose.

'What's the matter?' Scott asked.

'I did a . . . very bad thing!' Her English was hesitant, with a strong Italian accent.

Suddenly Scott figured it out. '*Gabriella*? Gabriella Moretti?'

She shrank back, glancing from side to side, like a rabbit faced with a hungry fox. 'How do you know this? You are police?'

'It's OK,' Scott told her. 'We're not with the police. We just know that you work as a cleaner here.'

'And that you saw Savannah Shaw in the manor on Monday night. The night she disappeared,' Emily added.

'I told lies!' Gabriella sank her head into her hands, which were red and chapped. 'A man gave me money to say those things.' She looked up, tears streaming down her face. 'I needed money. I was an *au pair* in Bristol, but the family was very bad to me so I ran away. But I want to stay in England so I work as a cleaner for now.'

'Who was this man?' Scott asked.

Gabriella shook her head. 'He did not tell me his name.'

'What did he look like?'

Gabriella frowned, searching for the words. 'Er, he is *round* . . .'

'Round? You mean fat? Like a walrus?' Jack asked.

'*Wal-rus*? I don't know this word.'

Jack puffed out his cheeks and waddled around clapping and making barking noises.

'That's a sea lion, you twerp!' Scott punched Jack's arm.

But Gabriella seemed to understand. She smiled for the first time. 'Oh! Yes, like a *wal-rus*!'

'Sid Golding!' Scott and Emily chorused.

Gabriella's smile faded and she stroked Drift's fur. 'I worked here last night but afterwards I told the driver I did not want to go back to Carrickstowe. I was frightened police would come for me. But now police are *here*. I think maybe that film lady is dead! And it is because of me.'

'No,' Emily said firmly. 'I'm sure Savannah Shaw

121

isn't dead. And none of it is your fault. You stay here and we'll go and find out what's happening.'

Gabriella began to cry again, this time with relief. 'Oh, thank you!' she sobbed.

—

The press conference wasn't hard to find. The excited buzz of voices led them straight to a large oak-panelled reception room at the front of the manor. The room was packed. Reporters were sitting in rows of chairs, but also crammed into the aisles and round the walls. Everyone was staring expectantly at a long table on a platform at the front of the room. Detective Inspector Hassan and two other police officers were sitting behind a bank of microphones, looking out across the crowd. Three other chairs at the table were empty.

Scott, Jack and Emily elbowed their way through the crowds with Drift sticking close behind. It was so chaotic no one noticed that the little dog had followed them inside. Scott bumped into a man with a goatee beard, who was obviously trying to remain out of sight at the back.

Neil Denton turned and recognized Scott. 'Welcome to the circus!' he said, taking off his glasses and wiping them with a handkerchief.

'D'you know what this is all about?' Scott asked.

Neil shrugged. 'Sid Golding's calling the shots. It's

not official but the word on the street is that Savannah Shaw has been found. Not sure whether she's been transformed into a zombie or a vampire,' he laughed, 'but apparently she's alive!'

Suddenly camera flashes began exploding in every direction. When Scott's eyesight recovered, he saw Sid Golding swagger out onto the platform. He shook hands with D. I. Hassan, lowered himself into the centre chair, took a drink of water and tapped the microphone. It squealed with feedback. 'Someone!' he yelled. 'Get me another mike!' An assistant hurried over and turned the volume down.

There was silence as Sid Golding stood up, placed the knuckles of both hands on the table and leaned forward. The room was stifling and there was a sheen of sweat on his face. 'As you are all aware, the last few days have been deeply traumatic for all of us who are close to Savannah Shaw . . . ' Jack tuned out for a few minutes while Golding burbled on about his *appreciation for the tireless efforts of the Cornish Police Force . . . blah blah . . .* He gazed around the room and noticed that several of the actors and other members of the film crew were in the audience too: Megan, Kenzo, Larry the bodyguard and Lauren O'Brien were all there . . . but, no sign of Max Fordham or Brett diBlanco.

'. . . it is my pleasure to inform you,' Golding continued, 'that Savannah Shaw was found at nine this morning, local time . . . ' Now Jack was listening. He exchanged glances with Emily and Scott. All around, there was a flurry of murmuring, chair-scraping and people hushing each other. 'She was found right here in Pendragon Manor, trapped by the curse of the ghost of Sarah Goodwell . . . '

Jack looked at D. I. Hassan. His monster moustache twitched and seemed to be hiding a smile. He raised a hand as if to silence Golding, but Golding ignored him and continued . . . 'Yes, there may be those among you who find it difficult to believe, but I assure you, we are dealing with a supernatural event. And Savannah Shaw was, indeed, rescued by her one true love . . . But, hey, enough of me, why don't we let the two lovebirds come in and tell the story in their own words . . .'

The excitement in the room was at fever-pitch. The reporters were on the edges of their seats, notebooks and voice-recorders poised. Cameras and mobile phones were held high, ready for the shot.

'It must be Max Fordham!' Emily whispered. 'That's why he's not with the rest of the film crew. He's backstage with Savannah. I *knew* those two were in love!'

'But diBlanco's not here either,' Scott pointed out. 'It could be him.'

Everyone else seemed to think so too. A murmur of *Brett diBlanco* was rumbling round the room, getting louder and louder like an approaching train.

Emily shook her head. 'Uh-uh! Remember the nose-wrinkle!'

'You're not buying this ridiculous fairy story, are you?' Neil laughed. 'Witches and ghosts! What's next? The seven dwarves?' But he was craning his neck to see the stage just like everyone else.

'*Breeeeeett diBlaaaaaancooooo!*' Sid Golding trumpeted, with the drama of a boxing compere announcing the arrival of the World Heavyweight Champion.

Emily's heart sank. *Brett diBlanco?* Savannah didn't love *him*! But here he was, strolling onto the stage, sporting a blue linen designer suit and flashing his whiter than white teeth in all directions. He stood centre-stage, soaking up the applause.

'And Miss Savanaaaaah Shaaaaaw!' Sid Golding bellowed.

The audience surged forward to catch sight of the actress. The tumult of voices grew louder. People began to clap and whistle.

'Where is she then?' Neil Denton asked no one in particular.

'Savannah Shaw!' Golding yelled, even louder this time. 'Savannah Shaw?' This time it was a question. He turned to Brett diBlanco. 'Where the hell is she?' The microphone picked up his words for all to hear.

DiBlanco shrugged. 'She was there a minute ago.'

Sid Golding sat down. Then he stood up again.

He opened and closed his mouth like a puffer fish. 'Someone!' he screamed. '*Someone!* Tell me what is going on here!'

Savannah Shaw had disappeared for the second time.

Sixteen

Another Disappearance

Total chaos broke out in the press conference when the audience twigged that Savannah Shaw was a no-show. People were running in all directions. Some were piling backstage to look for Savannah there, while others were streaming out into the hall. Mrs Bailey, the housekeeper, came running out of her office, shouting something about *a calm and orderly fashion*, but no one took any notice.

127

Scott grabbed Jack and Emily. 'Come on! Let's get out of here before we get mown down in the stampede!'

'What's going on?' Jack asked, as they hurried across the hall.

Scott shrugged. 'No idea. But I know one thing. Golding and diBlanco might have faked Savannah's *first* disappearance to get more publicity for the film, but they had nothing to do with *this* one! They looked as shell-shocked as everyone else when Savannah didn't step out on that stage. Brett diBlanco isn't *that* good an actor!'

They were about to duck into a corridor when Sid Golding rushed out into the hall, yelling at a man Scott recognized as Larry the bodyguard. 'What do you mean you *lost* her?' Golding screamed.

'She said she needed to go to the bathroom!' Larry was almost in tears. 'I couldn't exactly go in there with her, could I?'

'Idiot! You're fired!' Golding threw open the front door and glared out. Everyone stepped back as if he was a hand grenade with the pin out. Suddenly he yelled and pointed out across the garden. 'There she is! Someone! Stop her!'

The crowd charged out onto the terrace. Scott, Emily, Jack and Drift rushed out after them and saw the figure of a slim woman sprinting across the lawn past the maze, her long, dark ponytail swishing from side to side. She was wearing a floaty pink dress and when she turned to glance over her shoulder, her eyes were shielded by glamorous sunglasses.

The cry went up. 'It's Savannah!' Everyone began to run after her, like a pack of hounds in pursuit of a fox. The three friends stood on the steps between the stone lions and watched the chase.

'What is happening?' Gabriella shouted as she came running round from the back of the house.

'Search me,' Jack laughed. 'It's all gone a bit random!'

'But you don't need to worry about Savannah Shaw being dead,' Emily added, with a smile. 'Look!' She pointed at the figure of Savannah, who was halfway down the drive, still well clear of the pack. 'She's definitely alive. If she gets bored of acting she could always take up running.'

Savannah had now reached the car park and was diving headfirst into a waiting taxi. The taxi pulled away with a screech of tyres. Next moment, there was a frenzy of engine-revving and horn-honking, as hundreds of vehicles sped off after the taxi onto the road that led to the causeway and back to the mainland. Scott saw Golding's black Ferarri jostling for pole position with a red Porsche and a BBC van. It was like a scene from an Agent Diamond film.

'What do we do now?' Jack asked. 'Don't think we've got much chance of catching that taxi on our bikes.' Then he glanced down at Drift, lying quietly at Emily's feet. 'I'm surprised *you* didn't give chase, mate, seeing as you've got even more of a crush on Savannah than Scott!'

Scott was about to aim a sharp kick at Jack's ankle when he suddenly felt an enormous cog click into place somewhere deep inside his brain. 'That's because it *wasn't* Savannah!'

'So, who was it then?' Jack scoffed. 'Leonardo da Vinci?'

'It was her stunt double,' Scott said. 'Lauren's not as tall as Savannah. I *thought* there was something a bit different . . .'

Emily immediately realized Scott was right. *That's* why Drift hadn't shown any interest in running after Savannah. It hadn't been Savannah at all. It had been Lauren O'Brien in her Maya Diamond wig and the sunglasses Savannah always wore. 'Of course! It's Lauren's job to look like Savannah in the films, but she fooled everyone for real this time. Everyone except Drift,' Emily declared.

'But if that lady is *not* Savannah Shaw, then where is she?' Gabriella asked.

'That,' Scott said, 'is the million dollar question.'

'And the *billion* dollar question,' Jack added, 'is *why* is Lauren O'Brien running around pretending to be Savannah? If this is all part of Sid Golding's secret plan, I've totally lost track of where he's going with it.'

Emily shook her head. 'I'm sure Golding wasn't in on any of this. He looked like a stunned mullet.'

Gabriella looked puzzled. 'Sorry, what is *mullet*? Is same as walrus?'

'Yeah, pretty much!' Jack replied.

'I think Savannah arranged this herself,' Emily went on. 'She must've asked Lauren to act as a decoy to lead everyone off the scent. Meanwhile, she could slip away unnoticed . . .'

Jack was struggling to keep up. 'But why would she want to go off again? She's only just surfaced from her last mysterious disappearance!'

'Hmm. Usually when a girl runs away, there is a *man* involved!' Gabriella said wisely.

'Yes, that's it!' Emily punched the air. 'Of course! It's Max!'

Jack snorted. 'You and blinking Max Fordham!' He turned to Scott. 'I swear Em's in love with him herself. She's *obsessed* with the man.'

Emily ignored Jack's comment. It all made perfect sense. Gabriella was right. There *was* a man in the story and it definitely wasn't Brett diBlanco. Savannah had wrinkled her nose at *him*. But she'd smiled when she talked about Max, and didn't the film crew say they'd been seen together? Emily had known all along those two were in love. *Savannah had run off to be with Max Fordham!*

Seventeen

Drift Gets it Right

The remnants of the crowd – those who hadn't jumped into their cars and taken off after the taxi – began to meander back up the lawn towards the house. A few dazed-looking individuals emerged from the yew maze; it seemed they had accidentally wandered into it in the confusion of the chase and they'd been trying to find the way out ever since. Emily recognized Megan and Kenzo among them. She ran over to them.

'Oh! My! God!' Kenzo was crawling along the ground as if he'd barely made it out alive. 'It'll take years of therapy to get over that!'

'Have we missed all the excitement?' Megan giggled.

'Well, Savannah went off in a taxi, except it wasn't Savannah . . .' Emily paused. 'Let's just say it's a long story. Do you know where Max Fordham is?'

Megan thought for a moment. 'You mean Soldier Boy? Yeah, he was here earlier.'

'He got a call on his mobile,' Kenzo added. 'Just before Golding came out and did his big number on stage. Action Man was out of here like a bullet out of an AK47 – or whatever you call those big guns they use in the SAS.'

Kenzo and Megan staggered off in search of refreshments as Emily ran back to her friends. Gabriella ruffled Drift's fur, hugged Emily, Jack and Scott and thanked them all for their help once again.

Emily took out her mobile and phoned home. 'Mum, has Max Fordham checked out?'

'Yes,' Mum replied. 'He just came flying in a few minutes ago. He grabbed his bags and said he had to leave immediately due to "unforeseen circumstances". Maybe the SAS have called him back for a special operation or something. Shame! Such a nice man . . . Now, did you have fun camping?'

'Awesome! Home soon. Tell you about it then!' *Well, maybe not* all *about it,* Emily thought. *I'll probably skip*

*a few minor details like sneaking into the manor at night
and hiding in the haunted room ...*

'Well, that's that then!' Jack said. 'Savannah and
Max are in *lurrrrve* and they've run off together. End
of story! I wonder if there are any good cakes in the
kitchens that Vicky could put our way.'

Scott hesitated. He was *pretty* sure Emily was right.
And if Savannah was with Max, then good luck to
them! But what if Emily was *wrong*? It didn't happen
often, he had to admit, but what if Savannah *wasn't*
safely eloping with Max? Maybe there was another
reason for her second mysterious disappearance. If so,
she could still be in danger. 'Is there some way we can
check that Max and Savannah really are together?' he
said carefully, hoping Emily wouldn't bite his head off
for doubting her theory.

He needn't have worried. Emily smiled and nodded.
'Good thinking. It's bad form to close a case before
all the loose ends are tied up properly. So, let's think!
We know Savannah climbed out through a bathroom
window. No one saw her leave so the bathroom must
be at the back of the manor. Come on, there'll be
footprints!'

'Max is probably waiting for her somewhere with a
car . . .' Scott continued as they ran round to the back
of the house.

'Or a boat. We're very close to the sea,' Emily pointed
out.

'Or a helicopter,' Jack suggested.

'Yeah, right!' Scott laughed. 'This is reality, not an Agent Diamond film!'

—

They soon located a frosted window on the ground floor that looked as if it belonged to a bathroom. It was open, and just big enough for a slim person to climb through. But the ground beneath the window was a cobblestoned courtyard. An entire army could have marched across it and there wouldn't be any footprints. 'This *never* happens to the Famous Five!' Jack grumbled. 'Oh, well, back to Plan B. Anyone for cakes?'

Emily ignored him and surveyed the location, assessing the situation. The courtyards, vegetable gardens and orchards at the back of Pendragon Manor were surrounded by dense woodland. Savannah could have climbed over the low brick wall and headed off in any direction. There was no way of knowing which way unless she'd left a trail of breadcrumbs or something. *Yes! That was it! Not breadcrumbs, but it was a trail and it might work . . .* Emily delved in her shoulder bag and pulled out the blue silk scarf that Savannah Shaw had given her. She'd decided she would always carry it with her for luck. She waved it at Jack. 'We'll use this.'

Jack stared at her as if she'd flipped her lid. 'OK, so

we can't find any footprints, but at least we know how to *accessorise*!'

'Duh!' Emily laughed. 'I'm going to give it to Drift . . .'

'Hmm! I'm not sure it's Drift's colour,' Jack said.

Emily sighed. Sometimes she wondered: did Jack have to *work* at being so dim, or did it come naturally? But then again, he did have the *occasional* flash of genius, she supposed. She crouched down and held the silk scarf under Drift's nose. 'Where's Savannah?' she asked. 'Find Savannah, Drift!'

The little dog sniffed the scarf. He sat up, perked his left ear and twitched his nose. Then his right ear popped up to join the left.

'Find Savannah,' Emily coaxed.

Suddenly Drift was off! Nose to the ground, he bombed across the courtyard and along a cobbled path. When he reached the wall he scrabbled and whined until Emily lifted him over. His tale waving like a flag, the little dog galloped along a winding path through the trees. Emily looked at Scott and Jack. Then they all scrambled over the wall and sprinted after him.

The path came out in a clearing. Drift scampered to a halt and sat down in front of a thicket of brambles, with a Job-Done expression on his face.

'Hang on,' Jack panted. 'This is where we left our bikes this morning. Drift's just been following *our* trail in reverse!' He pulled his bike out of the bushes. Emily grabbed hers by the handlebars.

Scott looked for his bike but it had gone. 'I don't believe it! Someone's nicked it! It had Aunt Kate's tent on the back too.'

At the same moment, Emily noticed a scrap of paper tucked under her brake cable. 'What's this?' She unfolded it to find two fifty-pound notes and the words *This is for the bike. Sorry!* 'How strange,' she said, handing the money to Scott. 'Your bike, your cash!'

'Why couldn't they have nicked this pile of junk instead?' Jack said, kicking the old borrowed bike. I'd have taken a fiver for it, let alone fifty quid!'

Scott shrugged and stuffed the notes into the pocket of his jeans. He was annoyed his bike had gone but it was quite old and it hadn't been anything special – not like Jack's fancy BMX bike. He'd be able to get a decent second-hand bike with the money – although he'd have to give some to Aunt Kate for the tent too.

Emily looked down at Drift, who was still looking pleased with himself. She couldn't understand it. Drift had seemed so certain he was on Savannah's trail. He'd never been wrong before. Then she realized: Drift *wasn't* wrong. 'Savannah *was* here!' Emily exclaimed. '*She* took Scott's bike!' Emily bent down and cuddled Drift. 'Clever boy!' Then she looked around the clearing. There were several paths leading off in different directions. 'We need to see which way

Savannah went. Look for broken twigs and leaves . . . '

'Broken twigs?' Jack laughed. '*Hel-lo!* We're in the middle of a wood the size of Switzerland!'

'Alright, tyre tracks then!' Emily snapped. 'Look, you can see three on this path here. That was us coming from Westward Beach this morning. '

Jack strolled to the other side of the clearing, picked a path at random, knelt down and pressed his ear to the ground. 'Ah! Sitting Bull say film star pass this way,' he intoned in a voice like an Indian Chief in an old cowboy film, 'on iron horse with two wheels.'

Scott laughed and shoved Jack's shoulder. As he looked down at Jack rolling around in the dead leaves, Scott noticed a single track imprinted on the dried mud of the path. 'She *did* go this way.'

Emily ran over to see. 'Well spotted, Scott!'

Jack stood up and threw his arms out in protest. 'Excuse me! What about *well spotted, Sitting Bull?* Who led Scott to the right path in the first place?'

Emily laughed. 'Whoever found it, this path joins the road across the moor back to Castle Key.'

'But what does Savannah want to go to Castle Key for?' Jack asked. 'No offence, but there's not much there apart from the castle.'

'That's it!' Emily threw her arms around Jack in a bear hug. 'The *castle*! That's where they're meeting.'

Jack blushed. 'Hands off! Don't crowd the genius at work!'

'Let's go!' Emily said. Drift hopped into his basket.

'Er, just one problem,' Scott said. 'Savannah Shaw has my bike!'

Emily was already pedalling off down the path. She glanced back. 'Ask Sitting Bull for a lift!'

Eighteen

Close to the Edge

By the time they reached Castle Key, Scott was convinced he would never walk again. He'd taken turns with Jack – pedalling the bike and riding on the parcel rack – and he wasn't sure which was worse. He and Jack had threatened to kill each other so many times and in so many different ways, he'd lost count. At least it wasn't as hot as it had been; the sky was darkening with bruise-coloured clouds and a thick fog was rolling in from the sea.

The castle was deserted. It seemed everyone had downed tools and gone to the press conference to find out what had happened to their leading lady. The trailers and rigs, the booms and winches and platforms, all stood silent around the hulking outline of the ruined castle, rising out of the swirling white fog. Scott shivered. It looked like a ghost town, abandoned in the wake of an alien invasion or the Black Death.

The friends wandered round the castle. 'Max!' Emily called. 'Savannah!' Her words hung in the damp air. There were no replies. 'Looks like I was wrong,' she mumbled. 'They're not here.'

They were about to give up the search when Scott noticed a bike wheel poking out from behind a pile of boulders near the tower where Max and Lauren had been working on the stunts for the film. It was *his* bike! They all stared at it for a long time. Emily had been right after all, Savannah *had* cycled to the castle. But she and Max must already have left.

'We've missed them!' Scott said eventually.

⁓

'Well, that's that then. Case closed!' Jack kicked a stone and stuffed his hands into his pockets. 'Let's go. It's getting chilly up here. There's a hot chocolate with my name on it in Dotty's Tea Rooms.' He cupped his ear and pretended to hear something. 'Listen. It's calling me ... *Jack* ... *Jack* ... *I'm waiting for you* ... '

Drift stopped in his tracks and twitched his ears. Emily laughed. 'It's OK, Drift. It's only Jack goofing around!'

'What's new?' Scott said.

But Drift's ears were still standing to attention.

Maybe he's hearing something else, Emily thought. She strained her ears to listen. There was just the usual soundtrack of the island: gulls wailing overhead, waves breaking on the rocks below, Drift panting softly ... and then, so faint she wasn't sure whether she was imagining it ... a cry ...

'Help!'

Scott heard it too. He raked his floppy fringe back with his fingers and looked around, his grey eyes clouded with worry. 'Where's it coming from?'

Jack pointed out to sea. 'That way!'

Scott shook his head. 'It can't be! The fog must be distorting the sound. There's nothing there . . . unless . . .'

Emily didn't want to believe it either, but Drift's ears were pointing the same way.

'Help!'

Emily finished Scott's sentence. ' ... unless someone's fallen off the cliff!'

Jack ran towards the edge to look.

'Nooooo!' Scott yelled. He could hear Aunt Kate's

voice warning him and Jack on their very first morning in Castle Key . . . *Oh, and don't go wandering on the cliffs near the ruined castle . . . It's very dangerous where the ground is crumbling away . . .*

Jack turned. 'Someone's down there. We can't just leave them!'

'I know that!' Scott snapped. 'But it won't help *them* if *you* go over the edge as well, will it?'

'Scott's right,' Emily said. 'Stay back, Jack.'

Drift barked in agreement.

Now Jack thought about it he didn't *really* fancy base-jumping off the cliff-top without a parachute. He could see the place where the ground had fallen away, like a big bite out of a piece of shortbread. He took a few steps back.

'Hello!' he yelled. 'Is someone down there?'

'Help me . . . please!' came back a desperate cry.

Jack gulped as he recognized the voice. *It was Savannah Shaw!*

'Are you OK?' Scott called.

Jack rolled his eyes. *Of course she wasn't OK.* She was stuck on the side of a cliff, suspended hundreds of feet above raging waves and jagged rocks.

'I can't hold on much longer . . .'

'Savannah, we're going to help you!' Emily shouted.

Scott pulled his phone out of his pocket. 'I'll call the Coastguard. They'll send a rescue team.'

'Help . . . I'm slipping!'

Jack knew they were running out of time. The rescue team might be too late. They had to do something! 'Come on, there must be some ropes here somewhere.'

Without waiting for arguments, Jack ran to the tower and began gathering coils of rope. Emily joined him. 'Look for safety harnesses and carabiner clips!' he shouted.

'I saw Max put them in here.' Emily threw open a large metal trunk.

'Now we need something solid to tie the rope to . . .' Jack began searching for a post or pillar near the cliff edge to anchor the rope, but there was nothing. He could hear Scott nearby talking to the Coastguard. '*Fifteen minutes?* Hurry, please!'

From the panic in her voice, Jack wasn't sure Savannah could hang on for fifteen *seconds*, let alone fifteen minutes . . .

Scott ran to the platform the film technicians had attached to the side of the tower. He yanked on an upright scaffolding pole. 'What about this? It feels pretty solid.'

'But it's way too far,' Jack said. 'None of the ropes are long enough.'

'We can tie them together.' Emily grabbed two ropes from Jack's arms. 'A double fisherman's knot will do it,' she said, her fingers flying. 'Old Bob showed me this one years ago.' She held up the ends and pulled. 'No way that's coming undone.' She took another rope and repeated the knot. 'That should be long enough.' Then she tied the end of the rope around the scaffolding pole with a bowline. It was just like mooring a boat.

Jack considered his next move. If it was up to him, he'd abseil over the side and clip Savannah on to the rope himself, but he knew that Scott and Emily would never let him take that risk. He attached a second rope to the pole, pulled on a safety harness and tied himself onto the rope with a double figure of eight knot. He'd been through this routine hundreds of times before at the school climbing wall, but now his fingers just seemed to be fumbling around like sausages. It was taking forever.

Scott shook his head as if he couldn't believe his eyes. 'YOU ARE NOT GOING OVER THAT CLIFF!'

'It's *far* too dangerous!' Emily yelled.

Predictable or what! Jack thought. 'I'm not planning to go over. I'm going to lower this down to Savannah.' He held up the rope and tied a loop in the end. 'If she can grab the loop we can hold her weight until the rescue team gets here.'

'Please hurry . . . can't hold on . . . much longer!' Savannah's anguished cry floated up from the void.

Jack handed Scott and Emily the safety line attached to his harness. 'Hold this and take up the slack!' With that, he picked up the rope for Savannah and began to commando crawl towards the cliff edge.

'Savannah!' Emily shouted, 'Hang on! We're coming!'

Jack was very close to the edge now. He could feel the ground creak beneath him like thin ice. It was held up by little more than the roots of the coarse grass that grew on the cliff-top. Flattening his body to spread his weight he eased forward until his head and shoulders were over the precipice. A few crumbs of sandstone skittered down the cliff. For a dizzying moment he looked down into a nothingness of white fog. Then he made out the dark rocks far below. This was a long way from the climbing wall, with its colour-coded handholds and a nice soft crash mat! But he could feel the tension on the safety line attached to his harness. He wasn't going to fall. He forced himself to focus, and turned his gaze to the rock face beneath him.

Savannah was only about three metres down. Her right hand was clutching a tiny snag of rock. Her left arm was hugging the cliff face for balance, but there was no handhold. Jack couldn't see what her feet were resting on but it couldn't be wider than a paper clip. It was amazing she'd had the strength to cling to the sheer rock like a human fridge magnet for so long. But Jack could see there was no way she could hold on until the Coastguard arrived. Her body was shaking with exhaustion already.

'Savannah, I'm going to let this rope down next to your left hand. When I say, just reach out and grab the loop, OK?'

'Please . . . hurry . . .' Savannah's voice was barely a whisper.

Carefully, Jack fed the rope over the edge. It was vital not to let it slide down too fast. Even the tiniest knock could make Savannah lose her grip. And he didn't dare lean over further in case he caused the overhanging edge to collapse and sweep Savannah off the cliff in a landslide. But, at last, the rope was in place, so close to Savannah's hand that it was almost brushing her skin.

'Savannah, don't move yet. When I say so, stretch out the fingers of your left hand. The rope is right there. As soon as you feel it, grab it!'

'OK!'

'Scott! Em!' Jack called. 'Keep tension on the rope, ready to take her weight!'

'We're ready!'

Jack took a deep breath. This was the most terrifying moment of his life. There would be no second chances. It *had* to work! *'NOW!'*

'Aggh!' Savannah made a grunting sound as she tensed her body and reached out, her fingers feeling for the rope.

And then she fell.

Nineteen

Batman and Robin

Jack closed his eyes. He couldn't look.

'What's happened?' Scott yelled. 'Is she OK?'

Very, very slowly, Jack forced his eyes open.

Savannah was dangling from the rope by one arm. For a moment Jack thought he might actually pass out from pure relief. 'Yes!' he called. 'She's managed to get her wrist through the loop!'

'Thank goodness!' Emily dug her heels harder into

the ground and leaned back to take the weight. She hadn't noticed before but tears were streaming down her face. At that moment, she heard the rumble of a vehicle. She turned to see a jeep rattling towards them at top speed. It had driven straight through the car park and round the castle onto the cliff-top.

'It must be the Coastguard,' Scott said. 'We're over here!' he shouted.

But the man leaping out of the jeep and running through the mist was Max Fordham. 'Savannah!' he shouted. '*Savannah!* Where *are* you?' Then he caught sight of Scott and Emily. His flinty blue eyes followed the rope that led to Jack spread-eagled on the cliff edge. 'Savannah?'

'It's OK,' Emily said. 'She fell over the cliff. But we heard her calling for help. We've managed to get a rope to her . . .'

All at once, Max leaped into action. He raided the box of equipment and within seconds he'd hammered a series of metal hoops into the ground, attached a rope and clipped himself on. Then he was abseiling over the side of the cliff. Jack watched in awe as he looped a sling beneath Savannah and clipped her onto his harness. He began to climb back up the rope, using nothing more than a prusik cord tying his harness to the rope with a friction knot. He wrapped his foot in the rope to take the weight each time he slid the knot higher, and then pulled up with his arms. His tendons stood out like steel cables and his biceps bulged with the strain.

Jack backed away from the edge and sank down on the grass with Scott and Emily to watch as Max helped Savannah up over the lip of the cliff and then hoisted himself up after her. The two of them rolled away from the edge onto solid terrain. Drift thought it was a game. He bounced up and down on top of them, overjoyed to see Savannah again.

Savannah ruffled Drift's fur and kissed him. Then she sobbed into Max's shoulder. 'I thought you weren't coming!'

Max held her tight. 'It's OK, I'm here now. I had some reporters on my tail. I had to drive all over the island to lose them.'

'I was looking everywhere . . . It was so foggy . . . I didn't realize how close I was to the edge . . .'

Jack looked away. This was *way* too soppy for his liking.

Emily folded her arms and shot him a look he could only describe as disgustingly smug. 'Told you!' she said. 'Those two are so in love!'

Savannah sat up and unclipped her carabiner from Max's harness. One side of her face bore a fierce red graze. She looked like Maya Diamond after fighting off a gang of Dr Zoltan's hitmen – except that in the movie, her face would be flawless again by the next scene. She winced as she rubbed the rope burns on her wrists, but her sobs had turned to laughter. 'Emily, you are a *hopeless* romantic!'

'What do you mean?' Emily asked.

'Yeah, I *do* love Max. But not like *that*. We're friends . . . best buddies . . . *mates,* as you say in England.'

Emily stared in amazement. But she'd had it all worked out. 'Are you *sure* you're not in love?'

Savannah laughed again. 'Sure I'm sure! But, from the first film we worked on together, Max was the only one who ever treated me like a real person. And even though I'm never allowed to do my own stunts in the films, Max taught me them in secret . . . '

Max grinned. 'Good thing I did! Otherwise you'd never have had the upper body strength to hang on to that cliff-face.'

'And Max always sneaks burgers and fries up to my hotel room when I'm meant to be on a seaweed and grapefruit diet,' Savannah went on. 'Yep, he's my hero!'

'You hear that boys?' Max laughed. 'The way to a woman's heart is through her stomach.'

Savannah punched his arm. 'Sorry to disappoint you, Emily, but we're not quite Romeo and Juliet, I'm afraid.'

'More Batman and Robin!' Max laughed.

But Emily *wasn't* disappointed at all. Savannah and Max were *best friends* – just like she was with Scott and Jack. They were united by a love of dangerous stunts and fast food. And that was *way* more fun than the red-roses-and-love-hearts kind!

Max helped Savannah up and they all began to walk towards the castle. Savannah was limping slightly. Suddenly she stopped. 'Hey, what am I thinking? I haven't even thanked you guys for saving my life. Come here!' She engulfed all of them in turn in enormous hugs. Emily couldn't tell who was blushing more, Scott or Jack. They *both* looked like radioactive beetroot.

'I just remembered. I phoned the Coastguard,' Scott said, trying to regain his cool. 'They'll be here any minute!'

'Good call, mate!' Max told him.

But Savannah's face fell. 'Oh, no! If they come, the police and the reporters will be right behind them.'

'No worries, I'll get them to stand down.' Max pulled his mobile phone from his jeans pocket and informed the Coastguard that he was fully trained in Search and Rescue techniques and had everything under control.

They all flopped down on a big squashy crash pad at the base of the tower. The fog was beginning to lift and the sun was breaking through.

'So, what really happened?' Scott asked. 'You didn't *really* see the Midnight Ghost, did you?'

Savannah smiled and shook her head. 'No, sorry. Nothing that exciting! It was all a publicity stunt cooked up by Sid Golding . . . You'd think he'd be satisfied that the Agent Diamond series is one of the biggest box office hits ever! But he always wants *more, better, bigger*! He thought it would be good for the new film if I started dating my co-star, Brett diBlanco. And when he heard about the Midnight Ghost, he and Brett got this idea to spice the story up a bit. And, of course, it took the heat off Sid too. Some reporters have been taking a lot of interest in his business dealings lately, and this story took their minds off all that for a while!'

Emily grinned at Scott and Jack. 'We were right!'

Savannah's perfectly arched eyebrows nearly flew off her forehead. 'You mean you *knew* what was going on?'

'We weren't totally sure until after we'd interviewed Gabriella . . . ' Jack told her.

'Gabriella?' Savannah asked.

'Gabriella the cleaner,' Scott explained. 'She's the witness who was meant to have seen you near the haunted room when you first disappeared. But she told us Golding had *paid* her to say that.'

Suddenly Jack thought of something. 'Does diBlanco dot his "i"s with circles, by any chance?'

Savannah and Max stared at him with matching blank looks. Jack laughed. Now he thought about it, it probably did sound like a *slightly* random question.

'Er, yeah, he does,' Savannah said. 'He thinks it makes his writing look artistic or something. Why?'

'Oh, just that there were circles over the "i"s on the first note in the haunted room,' Jack explained. 'We got writing samples from the other suspects, but Brett wouldn't play ball and give us an autograph.'

Savannah whistled and shook her head at Max. 'And

I thought these guys were up here by *chance* when they heard my cry for help. I didn't realize I was under *investigation*!'

'The thing we couldn't work out was where *you* were while those two were planting all the notes and stuff,' Scott probed.

Savannah smiled. 'I was hiding out in a little cottage Sid rented for me near Truro. That was the main reason I went along with the whole stupid scam. I got a few days all to myself. I read books, watched movies on TV. I even went out to the shops a few times in disguise. It was heaven on a stick!'

'Is that why you decided to disappear the second time? At the press conference?' Emily asked.

'Yeah. I was meant to come out on stage, all lovey-dovey with Brett, with this stupid story about how he'd found me and broken the curse by being my one true love . . . '

'Pass the barf-bag!' Jack muttered.

Savannah laughed. 'That's exactly how I felt too. And then Brett started whining because the colour of my dress clashed with his suit! He is honestly the vainest, most arrogant . . . ' she paused, searching for the perfect word.

'Slimeball?' Jack offered.

Savannah clapped her hands. '*Slimeball!* You took the word right out of my mouth! So there I was, about to tell the world how much in love I was with a guy who's so in love with himself he probably kisses the bathroom mirror every morning! Something snapped. I couldn't go through with it. And I've been wanting to break out from the Agent Diamond films for a while now. I've done six of them already. It's time to move on. So, when I saw Lauren going into the bathroom, I had this crazy idea. I followed her in and asked her to help me. We called a cab to pick her up from the front of the house as a decoy. Then we swapped clothes . . . ' Savannah paused and looked down at her jeans. 'These aren't meant to be *cropped* jeans, they're just too short for me! Luckily Lauren had her Maya Diamond wig in her bag, so she put it on and then ran for it.'

'Meanwhile you climbed out of the bathroom window?' Emily prompted.

'Exactly. I called Max and asked him to meet me. The castle was his idea. I thought I was going to have to run all the way, but then I was in the woods and I found these bicycles just waiting – as if they'd been left there by magic!'

'Yeah,' Scott said. 'Magic!' He could still feel the bruises from riding on the back of Jack's bike, but he decided to let it pass. 'So what's the plan now?' he asked.

'We're running away together, aren't we?' Savannah poked Max in the ribs.

Max laughed. 'We made a pact years ago that if one of us got fed up we'd take off round the world on an Adventure Tour.'

'We're going scuba diving in the Caribbean!' Savannah said.

'Heli-skiing in the Alps,' Max added. 'Mountain climbing in Nepal. Hang-gliding in New Zealand . . . '

'Wow! Can I come?' Jack asked.

Suddenly they heard the revving of engines. A convoy of vehicles was roaring up Castle Road.

'Uh-oh!' Max groaned. 'That'll be the police or reporters looking for us. Or both. I guess they'll have figured out that they were following Lauren on a wild goose chase by now!'

'How are we going to get away?' Savannah asked frantically. 'We can't go back down the road without them seeing us. And I'm not going over the cliff again! Is there *any* other way down?'

Twenty

Escape from the Castle

'Max and Savannah could go down the secret passage!' Jack cried.

Emily shook her head. That had been her first thought too – the friends had discovered the tunnel from the castle down to the Whistling Caves during Operation Treasure. But the entrance was in the curator's office and that was likely to be firmly locked. And anyway, she had a better idea.

'You could go that way!' Emily pointed across the headland.

Savannah looked puzzled. 'But there's no road.'

But Emily had lived all her life on the island and she knew every last centimetre. 'There's an old track that goes all the way over the cliffs and comes out in Pirate Cove.' True, the track was deeply rutted and overgrown, but Max *was* driving a jeep and surely he'd done loads of off-roading in the SAS.

'But how do they get to the mainland from Pirate Cove?' Jack asked. 'Swim for it?'

'I'll phone Old Bob,' Emily said, 'and ask him to meet them at Pirate Cove with a boat and take them to the mainland. That way they won't be spotted driving across the causeway.' Emily knew she could trust Old Bob to help Max and Savannah – and to keep their getaway top secret.

Emerald eyes sparkling, Savannah turned to Max. 'OK, let's go for it!'

Max nodded. '*Who Dares Wins*, eh?'

Savannah began to run towards the jeep. Then she stopped and pulled an envelope out of her pocket. She held it out to Scott. 'I've written a note for the police to explain that I'm leaving of my own free will. I don't want them wasting their time looking for me any longer . . . but can you give us a bit of a head start?'

Scott took the note. 'Of course. We're so forgetful

it'll be tomorrow afternoon before we *remember* to give this to D. I. Hassan!'

'Hang on!' Jack said suddenly. 'Does this mean there'll be no more Agent Diamond films?'

Savannah laughed. 'I'm sure Maya Diamond will survive this crisis. She's a tough cookie! They'll find another actress to play her. After all, there've been seven different James Bonds! Or maybe I'll make another myself when I've had some time away.'

Max turned to the friends. 'Sorry, we'll have to take a rain-check on that rock-climbing expedition we were planning . . .' Then he saluted. 'You've done good work here today, guys. The SAS would be proud of you!'

Drift barked.

'And you too, Drift,' Savannah laughed.

Cars were pulling into the car park on the other side of the castle. 'You need to get going!' Scott urged.

Max took Savannah's arm and pulled her towards the jeep. 'Ouch, watch the arm, Max!' she cried. 'That's the one I use for dangling off cliffs!'

'Oh, you film stars are *so demanding*!' Max teased.

They were both laughing as they piled into the jeep. Max gunned the engine and they waved out of the windows as they bumped and bounced over the grass towards the track.

Jack waved back. 'Looks like their Adventure Tour has started already!'

Emily was on the phone to Old Bob. 'He'll meet

them there in half an hour,' she said as she finished the call.

Scott grinned and held up his hands. The three friends high-fived.

'Come on, let's get out of here before the reporters find us instead,' Emily said. They scrambled into the castle ruins, through a tumble-down archway and a gap in the wall, to the chamber hidden inside the tower that had been their HQ when they were investigating the stolen treasure. Emily flopped down on the grass, took out her notebook and started writing. 'I declare Operation Lost Star officially *SOLVED*!'

Suddenly Scott thought of something. 'I think we might have solved the Mystery of the Midnight Ghost into the bargain!' he said, gazing through an arrow slit out across the waves. 'You know how Sid Golding was trying to pair Savannah off with that slimeball, Brett diBlanco? I bet there were loads of girls in the sixteenth century whose families wanted them to marry some creep, just because he had money or land or something . . . Aunt Kate said that Sarah Goodwell was more of a matchmaker than a witch . . . Well, maybe she arranged for girls to have secret meetings with the guys they really liked. I bet the families just made all that stuff up about the girls vanishing at midnight to cover up for the fact that they'd run off with someone!'

'Ooh, so who's the hopeless romantic now?' Emily

giggled. 'I don't know if you're right, but it's a good story!'

'Never mind hopeless *romance*,' Jack grumbled. 'I'm starving! Being a ghost-buster, a genius *and* an action hero all in one day is hungry work! Who's for fish and chips at Dotty's?'

'I'm in,' Scott said.

Emily jumped up, squeezed out through the gap and took off at a run towards the bikes with Drift at her heels. 'Last one to Dotty's pays!'

Scott looked at Jack and bowed. 'After you,' he said.

Jack had almost reached his bike when he realized Scott was not trying to shove past and overtake him. That was *highly* suspicious! 'You not racing then?'

'I just remembered this,' Scott pulled the fifty-pound notes out of his pocket. 'We can't really give it back, can we? Savannah's probably bungee-jumping off Mount Everest by now. And I think she'd *want* us to spend it on fish and chips. Well, not *all* of it, of course.'

Jack laughed. 'Yeah. A hundred pounds' worth of chips might be a bit much, even for me! But she'd probably want us to have burgers and fries too. And she'd *definitely* want us to spend it on hot chocolates and banoffee pie.'

Scott looked down the road at the figure of Emily pedalling furiously down the hill. 'D'you think someone should tell her it's not a race any more?'

'Let's wait till we get to Dotty's,' Jack laughed.

Scott jumped on his bike. Then he stopped and patted the pockets of his shorts. 'Where's my phone?'

Jack grinned and held it up. 'I just borrowed it for a moment. I thought it was time to delete those stupid pictures of me before you got round to putting them on Facebook!'

'Give it back!' Scott lunged for the phone. He lost his balance and crash-landed in a crumpled tangle of boy and bike. Quick as a flash, Jack held up the phone and snapped a photo of his brother kissing the gravel with a bicycle wheel on his head.

'GIVE IT BACK!' Scott yelled again.

'Got to catch me first!' Jack hopped onto his bike and took off down the hill after Emily and Drift.

Don't miss the next exciting mystery
in the *Adventure Island* series

THE MYSTERY OF THE
HIDDEN GOLD

Available August 2011!

Read on for a special preview of the first chapter.

One

The Secret in the Cellar

N^{eed} *... somewhere ... to hide ...*

Jack hurtled down the spiral staircase three steps at a time.

There were some awesome hiding places in The Lighthouse. Emily had squeezed into an old trunk of ropes on the seventh floor. And they'd practically had to call in Search and Rescue to find Scott behind the old clockwork winding mechanism in the lantern room.

OK, Jack had to admit it *was* a good spot, but you'd think his brother had discovered life on Mars, the way he'd been gloating about it ever since. Which was why Jack *had* to find somewhere even better.

He paused on the fifth floor and glanced through the porthole window. A flash of lightning ripped through the swirling black clouds, lighting up the scene like an X-ray. Waves the size of double-decker buses were hurling themselves against the cliffs. The elements – sea, sky, rock, thunder, lightning – were slugging it out in an epic punch-up. And in The Lighthouse, they had ringside seats for the big fight! The breakers were crashing against the walls and the wind was rattling the window-panes. The storm was so violent that Emily's dad had switched on the lamp in the lantern room and the friends had only just made it inside without being swept off the promontory!

But right now Jack had more pressing concerns than the storm. Scott would probably have counted up to fifty already. In fact, knowing Scott, he wouldn't even have bothered to count. He'd just wait a few seconds, before shouting 'ninety-nine, one hundred, coming, ready or not . . . '

Where can I hide?

Jack hurried down the stairs, past the three floors of guest rooms – Emily's parents ran The Lighthouse as a Bed and Breakfast – past the kitchen on the first floor, to the guest lounge on the ground floor. Several of the guests were sitting around reading or playing board games. The storm had knocked out the main power supply, and although it was only late afternoon, the angry storm clouds darkened the sky. Emily's mum and dad had lit candles and the old wood-burning stove. The soft firelight flickered across the colourful rugs, sofas and wall-hangings that filled the huge circular room. The family who were staying at The Lighthouse for the week were playing Ker-plunk. A clatter of tumbling marbles was followed by a scream of *'That's not fair!'* and a squawk of *'He cheated!'* from the six-year-old twins.

Must focus on hiding . . .

The spiral staircase descended one more floor, to a cellar hewn deep into the rock. Jack had already hidden down there once, behind a rack of old lifejackets and oilskins, but it was worth another look. He grabbed a torch from a hook by the front door and headed down.

The cellar was cool. Jack shivered. The earthy scent of damp rock reminded him of the Whistling Caves, where he'd had to swim out underwater to escape the rising tide – not an experience he'd particularly enjoyed! That was not long after he and Scott had first come to stay with Aunt Kate while their dad was digging up bits of old pots in the middle of an African rainforest-slash-war-zone. The brothers had run into Emily Wild on their first day in Castle Key (literally: they were being chased by a stampede of cattle at the time!). Together the three of them had discovered a hoard of stolen Saxon artefacts in the caves, not to mention a secret passage to the castle. Since then, they'd also escaped from a haunted room *and* rescued a runaway film star.

No, this wasn't your *average* kind of summer holiday!

But, then, Castle Key wasn't your *average* kind of island . . .

Jack shone the torch around. The cellar was crammed with a random collection of crates and boxes and trunks. There were cases of wine, a box of canvases for Emily's mum's paintings, a set of golf clubs . . . Some of the stuff looked prehistoric! *Dad could probably get funding for an archaeological dig down here,* Jack thought. *But if I can just shift this ancient crate . . .* The crate was surprisingly heavy. *What's in this thing? Someone's collection of bowling balls and encyclopaedias?* But Jack was on a mission now. He shoved harder. Suddenly it budged.

Time was running out. This would have to do! But as Jack wedged himself behind the crate, he stubbed his toe on something hard. Cursing with pain, he shone his torch down. The culprit was a rusting iron ring. Curious, he gave it a quick tug. From beneath a carpet of dust, a wooden trapdoor creaked up out of the stone floor.

Ker-ching!

Scott and Emily wouldn't find him down *here* in a million years!

'OK, we give up!' Emily shouted. She looked at Scott. 'You don't think he's mad enough to have gone outside to hide, do you?'

'Mad enough?' Scott laughed. 'This is *Jack* we're talking about. Of course he's *mad* enough. He'd go surfing in a tsunami!'

That's what I was afraid of, Emily thought. 'He could have been swept out to sea in the storm . . .' She ran to the front door and pulled it open. 'Jack! Come back!'

'Shut the door!' A chorus of protests came from the lounge as a gale force wind roared through the room like an express train.

'No one has gone outside!' Mum shouted. She was playing Monopoly with one of the guests – a Japanese salesman called Mr Tanaka – and the wind had scattered her money all across the rug.

Emily sighed. *Where is Jack?* Drift – her pet dog, constant companion and partner in numerous investigations – was nudging his head against her knees. His black ear was standing up and his brown-and-white spotted ear flapped up and down. Emily knew he was trying to tell her Jack was in the cellar. She followed him downstairs – even though they'd already searched down there a hundred times. Drift was usually the ultimate sniffer dog, but this time the excitement of the storm must have fried his tracking circuits.

'*You're* going to have to say it!' Emily told Scott, after they'd scoured the cellar yet again.

'Say what?' Scott asked.

'That you give up, of course! Jack doesn't care whether I find him or not. He only wants to beat *you*.'

Scott groaned. Emily was right. But having to concede defeat to his younger brother was about as cool as doing up your top button and tucking your shirt in. Every fibre of his being was screaming, *Don't do it!* He swallowed, cleared his throat and squeezed the words out through clenched teeth. 'OK, I give in. You can come out now!'

'Sorry, didn't quite catch that!'

Scott whipped round. Jack's muffled voice was coming from somewhere close by but where *was* he? Had he found an invisibility cloak or something? 'I give in!' Scott uttered the dreaded words a fraction louder.

'Can I get that in writing?' Jack's grinning face appeared from behind a crate. Cobwebs smothered his spiky blond hair and dust smudged his cheeks like camouflage paint.

'But we looked behind there!' Emily gasped.

'I was down in that hidey-hole.' Jack stretched his arms. 'Phew, it's not exactly five-star accommodation, is it?'

'What hidey-hole?' Emily asked.

'The one under the trapdoor.'

'What trapdoor?'

Jack stared at Emily. 'You mean you didn't know it was there?'

Emily shook her head.

Oh, yes! What a result! Jack did a victory lap of the cellar. This was better than he could have hoped. He'd *only* found a secret hidey-hole that Emily didn't know about, right under her nose!

Together, they dragged the massive crate out of the way.

'Wow!' Emily breathed. 'I had no idea this hole was here . . .' She was about to carry out a full inspection when she noticed a roll of paper in Jack's hand. 'What's that?'

'Dunno! It was just lying on the ground down there.' Jack perched on the edge of a broken table and unfurled the scroll. 'It's got some old writing on . . .'

Emily and Scott pooled the light of their torches on the dog-eared sheet of yellowing paper. It was freckled with brown spots and the ink had faded to the colour of a tea stain.

'It's a letter!' Emily cried. She tucked her tangle of chestnut curls behind her ears and knelt down to examine the faint words. She made out a date at the top of the page: August the fifth, 1902. A shiver of excitement ran down her spine. *The letter was over a hundred years old!*

The three friends peered at the letter.

To Captain John Macy,
During the weeks that you have sheltered me here since you pulled me from the storm-tossed seas, I have come to regard you as a true and loyal friend.
For this reason I will now make known to you

*a secret of great import. First, I confess I have not
told you the full story of the terrible night that 'The
Empress' went down in the bay of Castle Key.*

*On that fateful night, I made my way into a lifeboat,
along with my fellow officer, Tommy Spring, and a
certain valuable cargo. In the teeth of the storm we
found ourselves thrown onto an uninhabited rocky
islet. Uncertain of what events lay ahead, we hid the*

'Hid the what?' Jack slapped his hands to his forehead.
'He can't just *stop* in the middle of a sentence. That's
mental cruelty!'

Emily's dark brown eyes gleamed. 'Ooh, I bet it was
contraband! Brandy or muskets or something.'

Scott and Jack looked at each other and laughed.
'Smugglers?' they chorused. Emily suspected *everyone*
of being a smuggler. If she hadn't already marked them
down as being a spy, that was! If the letter had turned
out to be a shopping list, she'd have been on the lookout
for a rogue grocer dealing in black-market baked beans
and Pot Noodles. But, Scott had to admit, there was an
outside chance she could actually be right this time.

A shipwreck, a secret of great import and something
hidden on a rocky island . . .

They'd been planning to play Cluedo next. But
Cluedo could wait.

They had a *real* mystery to solve now.

This letter had Adventure written all over it!